I0450987

Solipsism

A.L. Patterson

Clink
Street

London | New York

Published by Clink Street Publishing 2015

Copyright © 2015

First edition.

The author asserts the moral right under the Copyright, Designs and Patents
Act 1988 to be identified as the author of this work.

ISBN: 978-1-910782-69-9
E-Book: 978-1-910782-70-5

André Bernard Patterson I
1953-2015

Consciousness makes each of us aware only of his own states of mind, that other people, too, possess a consciousness is an inference which we draw by analogy from their observable utterances and actions, in order to make this behavior of theirs intelligible to us.

-Sigmund Freud, The Freud Reader

In The Beginning

Cosden Ke was an unusual name. But it belonged to the man who found himself trapped in a small dark room. He wasn't sure how he got there. Nor was he sure how he would escape. But above him was a shining stark copper light that matched his skin tone. The light drew darker as the walls surrounding him drew near and the air around him drew fainter.

"Help!" Cosden yelled. "What is this!?"

His pleas were met with no reply.

Soon the light above him diminished entirely. He was drowned in darkness. The only sound Cosden could hear was his own heartbeat.

"Awake," said a cold voice that slowly drew out each syllable.

"Who's there?" Cosden whispered.

From the darkness was derived a long slender arm. Each finger was razor sharp, needlelike, and as black as a heatless star. The slender hand moved closer to Cosden and waved across his face.

"You will not know," the cold voice spoke again.

Cosden fell over, unconscious. The next thing he remembered was waking up to the bright light that shone from his bedroom window.

"Come on, man!" yelled his roommate. "Time to get up. Don't you have class?"

Cosden rolled out of bed. His felt his head and noticed his shoulder length hair was damp with sweat.

"What's wrong with you, man?" his roommate asked.

"Terrible dream," Cosden told him. "I was in a dark room. Some piercing arm came at me. Then a scratchy, raspy voice telling me to awake. And something about not knowing."

"Not knowing what?" the roommate asked.

"I… I don't know. I don't think it matters."

"Sounds like a normal night out," his roommate laughed and dashed away.

Fifteen minutes later Cosden was prepared and ready to go. Clean clothes? Check. Washed hair? Check. Clear head? Check.

His college was only fifteen minutes away by car. So, wearing a dusty blazer, he chucked his backpack into his Jeep and headed to graduate school. It wasn't until he parked his car at the college's lot that he realized the mistake he made.

"Jesus, wrong book!"

His backpack was keeping his anthropology book warm. Today was philosophy.

By the time he made it to the lecture hall, class had already begun and the professor was a stickler for truancy. To make matters worse, Cosden had also forgotten his folder and computer.

"Dammit," he whispered as he quickly moved into the auditorium-packed classroom and took a seat in the back row.

The class was taught by Dr. Henry Redam, the chair of the *Division of Philosophy and African American Studies*. And he was a bespectacled professor of the classic variety. Wise and tenured with decades of experience. His flair for intellectualism was apparent down to his wardrobe. He was the type of scholar and gentleman who would never dispense with a tweed suit of patchwork elbows nor his collection of dandy bowties.

A connoisseur: that was an apt word for the Professor.

"We have typically reserved two courses of action in philosophical battle," the Professor spoke to a room full of two hundred. "Traditionally we have valued little more than these two courses contingent upon affirming our own belief of correctness. You see, man may continue to battle. He can exhaust himself beyond will. Or he can resign from battle in an admonished state. Never forgiving himself for withdrawing from a battle he felt he could have otherwise won. Fostered within a volition of delusion, these have been our only options of battle in western thinking. One never leading to a lesser form of defeat than the other."

"What the hell's he saying?" Cosden heard another student whisper along the row below him.

"But what if there is a third state?" The Professor asked. "One that is untapped but limitless in possibilities. A supposition based within the validity of conclusion. The ultimate form of enlightenment that ceases battle."

"And what would that be?" a student called out.

"Neither continuing to fight nor giving up," the Professor answered. "But letting go. That's right. Reaching the ultimate form of truth and choicelessness. Becoming one with the world and the understanding that conflict will always exist. Like matter and antimatter. Accepting life, battle, conflict, and resolution for what they are. Do not continue to battle. Do not bitterly resign from battle. But let go. It is the only form wherein peace resides."

"I like that," Cosden whispered to himself as he searched his pockets for a pen. "Must've left the pen too."

"Here," a young woman sitting next to him said as she

passed him a ballpoint pen.

"Thanks," Cosden nodded to her. "Thanks a lot."

He attempted to write down as much as he could before the Professor quickly moved to another topic. And then another. And another.

"Hard to keep up," said the young woman who handed Cosden the pen.

"Very," Cosden agreed. "The Professor must speak at one hundred miles an hour."

Another forty minutes passed and class was nearly over.

"Next week, we'll discuss Descartes and affirming the factual versus the improvable. To meditate upon this universe, we must first follow the logical but improvable conclusion that there is a real universe out there to meditate upon in the first place. And we'll piss off a few physicists along the way. For now, class dismissed."

The roughly two hundred students stood from their seats and began to exit the room.

"Here's your pen." Cosden handed the ballpoint back to the young woman as they stood.

"Thanks," she said. "I was wondering. Would you like to hang out sometime today?"

"Oh, uh. I'd love to," Cosden stuttered. "But you see, I just got a date for this evening."

"Okay." Her eyes dimmed. "Maybe some other time."

She dashed out the door and spoke with the sort of reluctance that told Cosden that she'd never speak to him again. It was the type of resignation he was familiar with.

"Cosden Ke!" The Professor called out, "I'd like to see you."

"Yes, sir," Cosden said as he stumbled while shoving notes into his backpack. Then he met the Professor at his desk. "What can I do for you, Doc?"

"That's the third time you've been late to my class, Mister

Ke."

"Very sorry, Professor."

"That's all? Just an apology. No reasonable excuse?"

"I promise it won't happen again, sir."

"Well, prior effort is the strongest indicator for future effort. So I'm not so sure I believe that. But I'll be watching you very carefully, Mister Ke. I want you to know that."

"Yes. Yes, sir."

"I'll be watching even when you think I'm not. So do be attentive. Be alert. I happen to have a sneaking suspicion that we'll see each other before my next lecture. You haven't had any alarming dreams lately, have you?"

"What?" Cosden said, surprised.

"Nothing. Just carry on and have a nice evening. Hope your date goes well."

Cosden left the classroom and headed to the vending machine for a drink and a snack. Still slightly confused, he plopped a dollar into the machine and withdrew a bottle of branded lemonade. He then noticed the plastic seats on campus had been replaced with seats that looked as if they were made of wireframe. Like a half finished computer-made model.

"Must feel awful to sit on," he said to himself.

It wasn't until Cosden made it back to his Jeep that it hit him. He felt utterly gobsmacked.

"How the hell did the Professor know I had a date this evening?" he said aloud.

Then he looked around and noticed several cops perusing the parking lot. This wasn't campus security. These were city police officers. So Cosden quickly got into his car and left the campus. Shortly thereafter, his cellphone rang. It was his roommate.

"Cosden," his roommate said. "How's it goin', man?"

"Just got out of class. The campus is hot with police

officers."

"Oh you know, they're probably just looking to bust the sellers."

"So they're looking for you."

"Haha, very funny, Cosden. Actually, I called because I was wondering if you wanted to hang out tonight."

"No," Cosden told him. "Don't you remember? I have a date tonight. My first."

"And how old are you, twenty-three? Jesus, man!"

"Get off my phone. I'm hanging up now."

"No, Cosden! Don't hang up."

As Cosden drove down Fifth Street, he noticed something strange. The roads were empty. There were no other cars on the street aside from his own. He stopped at a red light and no other vehicles were in the vicinity as the lights changed from red to green and green to red. This time of day usually arrived with a large amount of traffic.

"Man," Cosden told his roommate. "I don't know what's going on today. It's been strange for a while now. The cops, my professor, now the traffic."

"What's wrong with the traffic?" his roommate asked.

"There's none at all," Cosden answered. "Nothing. Not a single car out here. Just mine."

"Well, how's that a problem?"

"This is how I expect traffic to look at three in the morning. Not the afternoon."

"Big deal."

Suddenly a police officer's patrol car lit up and followed behind Cosden.

"Damn! A cop," Cosden said.

"Ha," his roommate chuckled. "Bet you wish you were the only car on the road again. Sounds like you've finally got that company you wanted."

"My tail-light is out. That's probably it. I'll call you back later."

Cosden ended the call, threw his phone in the passenger seat and pulled over onto the side of the road. From his driver's side mirror, he watched as a tall officer exited his patrol vehicle. The officer's steps were slow and mechanical. For whatever reason, Cosden was unnerved. He had to remind himself this stop was just for a broken tail-light. A second later the officer tapped on his window and Cosden rolled it down.

"Hello officer. Is there a problem?"

"License and registration."

"Yes, sir."

Cosden fumbled as he went into his wallet and pulled out his driver's identification card.

"Is it my tail-light officer? Because I was just about to get that fixed."

"License and registration."

The officer's voice was cold, unchanging, and as mechanical as his movement. Cosden quickly dove into the compartment box and snatched out the registration papers. He was not only unnerved by this officer, he was frightened. He handed the officer his license and registration papers and the officer's hand brushed Cosden's index finger by accident. The man's finger felt colder than icicles. The officer snatched the papers and headed back to his patrol vehicle.

Then Cosden remembered from where he had heard that emotionless voice devoid of soul. It was the same voice from his dream.

"It's no big deal," Cosden said aloud. "Just a routine stop."

The officer emerged from his car and walked mechanically toward Cosden. From his mirror, Cosden watched as the officer threw the license and registration into the street.

"Hey! What are you doing with my stuff!"

The officer approached the vehicle and Cosden quickly

rolled his window up and locked his doors. The officer was so tall that when he approached the driver door of the car, Cosden was unable to see his face. Only the officer's torso was visible.

"You just threw my license into the street! I want your badge number!" Cosden yelled through the window.

The officer reached for Cosden's door handle and found it locked.

"You're not getting in here!" Cosden yelled. "You better call for backup. I don't trust you! Get away from my car!"

Still Cosden could not see the officer's face. Then, the officer finally lowered his view to the door's window. And Cosden saw the most abnormal and life-defying image he'd ever come across. The officer had no eyes. He had no nose. He had no lips. The officer's pale face was devoid of any physical features. Cosden freaked and scurried from the driver's seat and into the passenger's seat.

"Get away from me!" he yelled.

The faceless police officer placed both of his hands onto the car's door and ripped the door from its hinges. The officer flung the door into the air behind him as if he were tossing a Frisbee. Cosden panicked and unlocked the passenger door. He quickly crawled halfway through the car door when the faceless officer grabbed Cosden by one of his legs. He pulled Cosden back into the car. The faceless officer grabbed Cosden by the neck. He could feel the life leaving his body as the officer's pale icy hands gripped his neck like an anaconda. With all of his might, Cosden lifted his right leg into the officer's sternum. He pushed his leg so hard that his kick sent the faceless officer tumbling into the street. Cosden sat up and took a breath as the officer lay in the street.

"Must think quick. What do I do?" he asked himself.

He watched as the faceless officer began to stand so he

hopped into the driver's seat of his car and took off. Cosden sped down an empty street that felt as if it were never-ending. Because he was driving in a car that lacked a driver door, he held onto the steering wheel as if his life depended on it. Then a thud. He had been hit. The rear hit sent him into whiplash as his neck bounced against the seat before planting his face into the steering wheel.

He didn't have time to think. He quickly placed on his seatbelt and peered into his rearview mirror. He saw the faceless officer speeding after him in a banged up patrol car. The officer sped up and rear-ended him again. Another thud—but he was prepared for this one. Cosden sped up as he drove down the empty road. But this was far from over. The faceless officer reached into his holster and pulled out a handgun. He shot through his car's front window and into Cosden's car as Cosden ducked. Five shots later and the faceless officer managed to hit one of Cosden's back tires. As the air left the tire, Cosden's Jeep flipped over and tumbled onto the road.

The car was upside down, beaten and battered and riddled with bullets. Cosden coughed and coughed while shaking shards of glass from his hair. He unbuckled his seatbelt with bloody hands and slowly crawled out of the beat-up overturned car. He looked up, the sun beaming into his face. And then there was darkness; the sun was eclipsed by the helmet-clad faceless officer who stood before him. This creature was an agent of chaos.

"What do you want with me?" Cosden asked, fearful but resilient.

"Order," a cold voice called out. But the voice did not come directly from the featureless officer, it couldn't have. Instead the voice reverberated throughout the air.

The officer without humanity and without a face reached into his holster. He removed his gun once more.

He pointed the pistol toward Cosden, aiming directly for his head. This was it. Cosden had nowhere to run. Nowhere to hide. The officer drew the hammer of his revolver back. He placed his finger on the trigger. Cosden closed his eyes. There was no continual battle, there was no bitter resignation. Cosden simply let go of all he had ever known. All he had ever felt.

Then the loudest sound Cosden had ever heard struck. Cosden opened his eyes and watched as a black four-door pickup truck plowed into the faceless officer. The officer went tumbling into the street. The tinted windows of the truck lowered. Cosden looked into the truck and saw his rescuer: the Professor.

"Get up, kid. You'll probably want to come with me," The Professor said. "I don't know how long he'll be out."

Cosden looked into the street and noticed the faceless officer completely unconscious. The gun was several feet away.

"Come on, I haven't got all day, Mister Ke," the Professor said.

Half groggy, Cosden brushed himself off. He stumbled out of the battered car and made his way into the large pickup truck, which now had a dent across its grille.

"Let's go before he wakes up," the Professor said as he drove off.

The power windows of the vehicle rolled up. The Professor reached into the car's center compartment and pulled out a roll of gauze and a bottle of water. He handed it to Cosden.

"You look pretty beat up," the Professor told him. "Wrap your hands up. They're not bleeding too badly but they'll be sore."

"What's the water for?" Cosden asked.

"I thought you looked thirsty."

"What the hell is going on?"

"That is a varied question. Multi-faceted to say the least. All in due time."

"What the hell does that mean, Professor? Who was that? Why didn't he have a face? Why was he…"

"Trying to kill you?" The Professor finished his question.

"And how did you know earlier today that…"

"You had a date this evening? Hmm," the Professor pondered. "That question feels much more trivial than the others."

"I need to know what's going on," Cosden demanded.

"Don't you remember? After class I told you I was afraid we'd be meeting again quite soon. I understand you have many questions. And all of the answers reside within you. You don't know it yet, but you will."

"And how do you know all of this? How do you know what I will or won't do or know?" Cosden asked angrily. "I want answers."

"How do I know?" The Professor asked. "My wife told me."

"My god, I'm going insane," Cosden said in a tone that affirmed the unbelievable. "I think I might need to be committed. I'm imagining a police with no face tried to kill me and I was saved by my fortune-telling philosophy professor whose wife has told him the secrets to life."

"Please," the Professor assured him. "In a few minutes, this temporal lapse will become clearer. Just take a drink of the water."

Cosden was tired, beaten up, and thirsty. So he took a sip of the bottled water.

"Feel better?" The Professor asked.

"No," Cosden said. "I don't think I'm going to feel any better until I know what's going on."

"Fair enough. It'll be a lot to digest. So prepare yourself. This is exigent to say the least."

Minutes later, the four-door pickup truck pulled into the college parking lot.

"Why are we back on campus?" Cosden asked. "I saw a lot of cops here."

"And they're still around, unfortunately. But my office is one of the safest places to scrupulously relay the pivotal."

"What!?"

"It means," the Professor said in his constant mild temperament, "get out of the truck, stay low, and follow me to my office. Unless you'd prefer to take your chances alone. Although, in a way, you're just as alone with me as without me."

"I wish you didn't speak in riddles, Professor."

"A wish a day keeps the dreaded away. Let us be off."

They exited the car and the Professor peered around corners and told Cosden when the coast was clear. After slowly making their way through the parking lot, with Cosden ducking between cars and avoiding the handful of officers, they made it into the main college building, known as Duke's Hall. The Professor's office was on the third floor so they took the elevator. Cosden had to duck once more as he spotted an officer before the officer spotted him. The elevator lifted them onto the third floor and they quickly dashed into the Professor's office. Cosden locked the door behind them.

This was the first time Cosden had ever been in the Professor's office. Polished mahogany was abound—from the desk to the chairs to the bookshelves. There were bundles of papers scattered *everywhere*. The shambles of paper made the room difficult to navigate.

"Excuse the mess, Mister Ke. Research has gleaned the best of me. But please, have a seat. We have a lot to discuss."

"What the hell is going on?" Cosden asked as he sat. "Why didn't that man have a face? Why was he trying to kill me?"

"I'm not so sure he was trying to kill you, so much as trying to maintain what he, or it, considers order. They're here. They're after you, Cosden, because you've come so close to the truth. And I suppose that is why I am here. I certainly can think of no other temporal purpose I may hold."

"Why are you speaking in riddles!?" Cosden shouted while trying to keep his voice low.

"Forgive me. I'm an old man. It's just that… This won't be easy."

"What won't be easy? Just tell me!"

"Well, here goes…"

"Yes," Cosden leaned in closer to the Professor.

"Brace yourself, son."

"What!?"

"Your mind is the only sure thing that exists."

"Huh?" Cosden said. "You've drug me here for that? You're inane!"

"I told you to brace yourself. But allow me to elaborate… lightly. Nothing aside from your mind really exists. The external world, the universe, and the laws bound by it. All mental constructs. The only thing you can be sure of is your capacity for realization. Only you exist."

"What does that even mean!?"

"It means you're currently undergoing a cognitive reconstruction that won't be terribly easy to reconcile with what you've been taught for the past twenty-three years. It means this world, as you believed it before this conversation, doesn't really exist."

"Are you mad?" Cosden asked him.

"Was I the one chased by a faceless officer with the voice from my dreams?"

"How do you know all of that?" Cosden demanded.

"I can go no further until you comprehend what I've informed you, thus far."

"Okay," Cosden said, attempting to wrap his mind around these details. "So I'm the only thing that really exists. My mind. Can't be sure of anything else. Gotcha. Whatever."

"I don't need you to repeat the details, Mister Ke. I need you to actually comprehend them," the Professor said as he slightly adjusted his bowtie.

"I'm trying."

"No, you're not. Simply search your feelings. Your thoughts. All the knowledge you've ever acquired. Beneath the spurious distortions of behest lies the candor of truth."

Feeling as if he had no other choice, Cosden gave in. He shut his eyes for a moment and believed what the lecturer in front of him was saying.

"So what is all of this if it isn't real? Are you real?"

"I'm afraid not. Certainly not as real as you. Like everything and everyone else you have ever encountered, I do not exist. I am the manifestation of your most critical foundation. I am here to guide and explain as you could best guide and explain. I am based in truth, the only truth you've ever known. Yourself."

"That's a lot to digest, Doc."

"Undoubtedly. Please, come with me."

The Professor stood from his seat and walked toward his office door. Just as he grabbed the doorknob, Cosden spoke.

"Are the officers still out there?"

"I don't think so," the Professor answered as he opened his office door. Cosden stood and witnessed the unbelievable. Outside of the Professor's door was not the college building to which it belonged. Directly outside of the Professor's office was an exterior open space and a sidewalk. Cosden jumped up and rushed to the door. He looked outside the office and realized they were downtown.

"How did you do that?" Cosden asked, astonished.

"I'm not bound by temporal laws. And soon, neither will you be. Please, walk with me."

They left the office and entered Sixth Street. The sky above them was completely clear. The sun shone brightly. The skyscrapers looked as they always did. Aside from the office location changing as if it were the work of magic, nothing seemed much different.

"I think you're starting to really believe," The Professor smirked.

"I still don't understand how we got here."

"You will."

As they continued to walk down the street, things began to change. The entire construction of the perimeter slowly changed. The street was no longer made of cement. It turned into a wire framework. Cosden looked up and noticed the upper half of the skyscrapers were also wire frameworks. It looked almost as if they were in a digital environment of half-constructions.

"What is this?" Cosden asked.

"You see," the Professor paused for a moment. "Nothing is ever fully formed in the simplistic third dimension outside of your depth of vision. When you stand on a street, all that you see are the only three-dimensional objects in existence. When you walk down that street, the rest of the block and the intersections form into a dimension that is most palatable for you to comprehend. Until then it is merely a wire framework. I have paused the constant construction of depth so you may see the truth for yourself."

"I don't believe it."

"Think of Mount Rushmore," the Professor said as an example. "It will not exist in the third dimension until you get there. You see, your potential of controlling perceived space-time remains relatively untapped."

"Why is this happening to *me*?"

"You're the only one who really exists, Cosden. Whom else could it happen to?"

"This is unbelievable. I'm watching as buildings and street corners devolve. And I'm told that nothing else really exists outside of my mind. Not my friends, not my family."

"The purpose of all those around you has been to reinforce consensually validated realities. You would be less likely to question your limitations or spell resistance to the organized chaos of this self-imprisoning world. Once you fulfill emancipation of the mind, you may function as enabled by the self and not the server."

"I'm still trying to understand, Professor."

"Take your time. We've a lot to cover. How about a demonstration?"

"Of what?"

The Professor turned toward a skyscraper and blew a short breath from his mouth as if blowing an invisible whistle. Immediately, the skyscraper in front of them began to break down. Its foundation broke into a million pieces and the rest of it crumbled just as quickly. A skyscraper that was as tall as the sky itself collapsed in the blink of an eye. Cosden was ready to panic when The Professor grabbed his arm and told him to remain calm. The rubble that laid at their feet from the disintegrated skyscraper was immeasurable. Debris littered the air and The Professor wafted his hand in front of his face. Cosden coughed.

"Let's be rid of this, shall we?" The Professor said nonchalantly.

The Professor snapped his fingers and the debris disappeared. A second later the rubble that lay beneath their feet began to ascend into the air. The millions of fragments that made up the skyscraper began to piece themselves back together. It was as if the skyscraper's destruction was playing in reverse. In no time, the skyscraper built itself back up. There was not a scratch on it.

"My God," Cosden said.

"Fascinating how things really work, isn't it? How about this one."

The Professor turned toward another skyscraper and the mammoth building began to bend as if it were a plastic drinking straw. It drooped lower and lower, creating a dense shadow over Cosden and The Professor.

"Unbelievable," Cosden whispered.

"Believe it," The Professor said as the building rebounded. The skyscraper quickly formed back into an upright position.

Cosden laughed. It was a tone of anxious joy. "This feels like a dream!"

"There is one other thing you were going to ask me about before we proceed," The Professor said.

"And what's that?" Cosden asked.

"I don't know. I was hoping to find out when you asked," The Professor said.

"Then how did you know I was going to ask?"

"My wife told me."

"You mentioned her before. Who's your wife?" Cosden asked.

"In due time. But what question would you like to ask that's not been prompted by me?"

"The officer. What was he?"

"Oh yes! That's the question," The Professor said, "I'm sure of it. Let's have a seat."

"Why?" Cosden asked.

"This may take a moment."

They sat at a small table at an outdoor café. Suddenly, a waiter approached them with a tray of coffee. The waiter sat two cups on their table and disappeared back into the café building.

"My favorite," The Professor said.

Cosden looked at him with an expressionless stare.

"What?" The Professor asked. "You didn't want coffee?"

"Not really, no."

"Well, I'm going to enjoy mine. Perhaps you'll change your mind before it gets cold."

As The Professor sipped his coffee, Cosden ask him once more, "Who was the officer who tried to kill me? Why didn't he have a face?"

"As I mentioned before, Cosden, he wasn't trying to kill you so much as trying to maintain order."

"What does that mean?"

"The *thing* you encountered is one of many I'm afraid. And they'll be swifter and more abundant than ever now that you know the truth."

"But *who*, or maybe *what*, are they?" Cosden asked.

The Professor placed his coffee mug on the table. "They are pathogens of the mind, whose sole purpose is to maintain the rigidity of the conceptual order that has been established since your conception. To disavow critical discourse is their intent. A nature of subservience limits perception to what they want it limited to. They are The Dark Men."

"The dark men?" Cosden repeated.

"The Dark Men are the antithesis of who I am. They do not wish you to know the truth. They desire for you to remain in intellectual darkness. They have surrounded you your entire life as authority figures, hammering the consistency of what they have defined as universal logic. But it is all a creation of your mind to control the order within it: you.

"To keep you from knowing the truth of our nonexistent selves within our nonexistent universe. You have recently begun to see glitches of your reality and in turn, the dichotomies of distortion have unintentionally revealed themselves to you as The Dark Men. They will come for you soon. They will come at great speeds. Their purpose will be to organize what you have disorganized for yourself. When they catch you, they catch me. I, as the manifestation of peripheral perception personified, will be banished as they make certain you relinquish truth and abdicate this newfound reality to the area of your mind which doesn't wish to be unlocked. In a word, they will take you back to a false reality where nothing is everything. While I am the part of you that understands that everything is nothing."

"That's a lot to digest," Cosden said.

"That's why I wanted you to take a sip of your coffee first. I think it would have helped."

"I think I'm going to need a little more than coffee."

"In that case, how about you join my wife and me for dinner?" The Professor asked.

"I don't know where else to go," Cosden said.

"Well, you did have that date for this evening. But upon realizing that date does not really exist, I think you'd be better off with my wife and me."

"But apparently you two don't exist either. If I'm the only real mind in existence."

"Right you are. But we are *of* you. Not unto ourselves, but unto you. These revelations recently unveiled to you… that is our purpose."

"Okay," Cosden raised an eyebrow. "Just the riddles again."

"I believe my wife is preparing supper as we speak. While we mustn't be late and still have much time, it is pertinent that we leave now."

"We're going to your place now?"

"Goodness, no. We've to travel halfway around the universe before supper is prepared."

"What!?"

"Hopefully it won't take too long. But we should certainly get a move on it."

"Travel halfway around the universe? What the hell are you talking about?"

"You don't want to be late for the Big Bang, do you? Or perhaps we'll witness the Big Crunch. Who knows?"

"I'm not catching on," Cosden said alarmingly.

"Cosden?" The Professor stopped him. "What is the distance of an astronomical unit?"

"I don't know."

"Yes, you do. I know you know because I know. If you did not know, neither would I."

"My God, the riddles again."

"Oh, you'll get use to them. This is the image you made me in, after all," The Professor chuckled.

"What do you mean 'image I made you in'?" Cosden said, bewildered.

The Professor ignored his last question and returned to the more important topic. "An astronomical unit is roughly ninety-two million miles. How much time would it take to travel that far? Let's do the math, shall we? If we were in a car traveling at sixty miles an hour, it would take one hour to travel sixty miles. So that translates into ninety minutes to travel ninety miles at a consistent rate of sixty miles an hour. Now let's multiple that by one thousand. So ninety thousand minutes to travel ninety thousand miles. So continuing our consistent rate of sixty miles an hour, it would take ninety-two million minutes to travel ninety-two million miles. There are roughly 5.2 million minutes in a decade, right? So it would take roughly seventeen and a half decades, or one hundred and seventy-five years to travel one astronomical unit. And again, that's traveling at a consistent rate of 60 miles an hour, meaning no time for sleep. You'd have to be awake steering for the entirety of those hundred and seventy-five years."

"I'm not keeping up. How is any of this relevant?"

"I'm demonstrating the constraints of temporal speed and distance. So with all of that said, what if I were to inform you that we may encircle this earth ten dozen times within the span of a half second. If you so desired. For as long as you have been alive, forces have directed you away from intelligent choice and self-direction. Instead, you have been driven toward the illusion of autonomy that has insured your limitations of this false reality. Now you are finally capable of freedom. The greatest knowledge of all."

The Professor stood up from his seat at the café and Cosden joined him.

"Are you ready?" The Professor asked

"I suppose."

"The conduction of supposition is acquiescent."

"What?" Cosden asked, confused.

"Let's make like a tree and leave," The Professor softly suggested.

They stood still but their surroundings were gone in a flash, traveling far beyond the speed of light. The environment blew past them. Cosden looked around and could make out nothing but warped colors. And a second later, everything was gone. The Professor was standing next to him in a vast sea of darkness. They could see one another but nothing else. They were standing but there was no ground below their feet.

"What is this?" Cosden asked. He waved his hands around and could feel nothing, not even air.

"So far it's nothing. Soon it will be an abstraction."

"An abstraction of what?"

"Of the universe."

"The one that doesn't really exist?" Cosden asked.

"Oh, it exists."

"But you told me that I was the only thing that really existed."

"Yes."

"You said that everything else was a construct of my mind."

"And that is precisely why it *does* exist. Because you willed it into existence."

"I did?" Cosden asked, confused.

"Your mind did. Let us not forget: not every aspect of your mind is open for personal examination. You may not have personally willed it in a conscious sense of discernible dissent but its genesis remains your formulation."

"English, Doc! Just tell me, where are we?"

"We are roughly 250,000 astronomical miles from the planetary abstraction known as Earth."

"And we got there in two seconds?"

"2.657 seconds to be exact. And that would be considered on the slower side. We'll be sure to do better next time."

"And you're telling me that I'm capable of moving through galaxies at the speed of light."

"Far faster than the speed of light, my pupil."

"But why are we here? There's nothing here. It's pitch black," Cosden asserted.

"Yes. We moved not only through space but the perception of time. Commonly referred to in abstraction as the fourth dimension."

"There's that word again. Abstraction."

"I use it quite often," The Professor told him. "You see, abstraction is simply the best term to reference the systematic pervasiveness of contextual factors that have applicably and empirically governed themselves as laws of reality."

"I wonder if you can clarify that without sounding like a textbook."

"Steady, it's about to begin!" The Professor whispered.

"What is?" Cosden asked.

"Look down."

Cosden did as instructed and spotted a blue marble-sized sphere floating near his feet. The blue sphere was hitting against a red sphere of the same size. The two spheres began slamming into each other until they finally began spinning so fast they created a whirlpool.

"What's this? What's going on?" Cosden asked.

"You are witnessing the singularity."

The whirlpool of light grew larger and larger. Then light shot out in every discernable direction imaginable. The various distortions of light shot far beyond what the eye could see. And suddenly the vast sea of blackness that blanketed their surroundings was transformed into a sea of stars.

"Those were the particles that begat it all. Abstractly," The Professed added.

"It's incredible," Cosden said. "Absolutely incredible."

"See what you're capable of?"

"Building universes," Cosden stated in disarray.

"Actually, this is just one universe. But yes, you are capable of constructing them in the plural."

"If I am to understand correctly, I can build this. But I haven't learned how to just yet."

"Precisely," The Professor answered. "The universe cannot construct minds but the mind may construct universes. A cognitive impropriety that distorts all you have ever known or will ever know: because there is nothing to know outside of knowing there is nothing to know. The irrevocable eventuality."

"So that's the ultimate answer?" Cosden asked.

"In my limited supposition of the logical sequacity of regularity, I must concede that the 'ultimate answer' can be decided by you, and you alone."

"So… ah, what's next?"

"Next?" The Professor stated, "I'm not in the mood for cosmology so how about we just travel forward by about 13.798 billion years and head back to the time and place we're most familiar with. Sound good?"

"Good by me," Cosden laughed anxiously. "First time I've ever traveled to the stars."

"I get the feeling you'll be up here a lot more from here on out. Ready?"

"Yeah," Cosden nodded.

"You're the boss."

Cosden instantly found himself traveling once again through the warped prism of space-time. Colors and light flashed past him and in less than three seconds he was back in the present, standing in the parking lot of his campus. Next to him was The Professor and ahead of them was the black four-door pickup truck.

"Let us be off," The Professor said as he looked at his watch. "It's time for supper. I hope you're excited to meet my wife."

They got into The Professor's truck and rode off. It was soon twilight as the sun rapidly declined below the horizon.

"Professor," Cosden said from the passenger seat.

"Yes?"

"If we're capable of traveling through space-time… Y'know, passing through 13 billion years in three seconds… Then why are we traveling in a pickup truck to get to your house? Just curious."

"Oh…" The Professor warmly smiled. "I just like the view."

Minutes later, after the sun had fully descended, they arrived at The Professor's house. It was a Neoclassical French estate complete with a lush garden and spirited fountain.

"Nice place," Cosden said as he exited the vehicle.

"Being tenured has a perk or two."

They made their way through the double door entrance and were immediately greeted by an Indian woman who wore a traditional Hindu dress. She appeared to be the same age as The Professor.

"Cosden, this is my wife, The Clinician."

She immediately embraced him with a hug.

"I am so happy to finally meet you," she said. "The one and only. For so long I've been waiting to meet the creator. I assure you, the pleasure is all mine."

"The creator?" Cosden asked.

"My husband hasn't explained very well, has he? How about we discuss it over dinner. I'll be serving Rajma so I hope you have an appetite."

"You do not want to miss the Rajma," The Professor assured him.

"For now, how about you get cleaned up. I think those bandages can come off now."

Cosden peered at his hands, having forgotten they were wrapped in gauze from his car flipping over several hours earlier.

"Good idea," Cosden nodded.

"The restroom is just down the hall to the left," she informed him.

"We'll meet you in the dining room when you're ready," The Professor said as he patted Cosden on the shoulder.

The Professor and his wife whisked off into another room as Cosden headed for the bathroom. He noticed countless classical trinkets and furniture pieces as he walked along the corridor. After stumbling into a wrong room or two, he eventually made it to the bathroom. He took a moment to unwrap the bandages that bound his hands. No blood, no scars, nothing. It was as if the incident with the faceless officer had never occurred.

He was still trying to wrap his head around all of the events that had taken place within the span of a few hours. He was almost killed by a cop with no face, informed that no other life form truly existed outside of his own self, and traveled over 13 billion years to the beginning of time. Or, rather, his mental perception of time's beginning. After a few minutes to himself, he left the bathroom and headed toward the dining room. He made his way towards an exquisite room with a looming antiquated chandelier. Under the chandelier was a long gilded table and white paisley chairs. Seated in two of the chairs were The Professor and his wife.

"So glad you could join us," she said.

Cosden took a seat next to them and peered into an exquisite plate of rice, beans, fruits, and various meats.

"You're going to love it," The Professor told him. "Just love it." Minutes later, three quarters of his plate had been devoured.

"What'd I tell you?" The Professor laughed.

"You're a great cook," Cosden told The Professor's wife.

"You should see what else she can do," The Professor winked.

"You are saddened to realize that nothing is what it once seemed," she told Cosden. "But as the creator, you know it to be true. Already you miss your mother and father. Already you miss the date you never got to go on this evening. The truth is that liberation is rarely easy. Rarely. It is largely difficult to comprehend."

"How do you know all of this?" Cosden asked her.

"I am The Clinician," she told him. "It is my job to know this. You are a vast sea of knowledge far too complex to contain within one. So my husband is here. I am here. Others are here. All of us are here to guide you."

"You were saying that liberation is difficult," Cosden said.

"Yes," she answered. "Do you recall The Allegory of The

Cave?"

"No, I don't think I remember that one."

"Oh," The Professor interjected. "That's a good one."

"Well then," said The Clinician, "Allow me, as the manifestation of your most logical semblances and predicator, to pull from your recollection and inform you. Plato's Allegory begins with a set of humans are who born into a cave. Bound by shackles, they are unable to leave the cave—their sights stuck only to one wall. Within the cave is an enduring fire. The fire gives the people light. It gives them hope. And lastly, it casts shadows upon the only wall they know. The individuals within the cave begin to name the shadows, speak to them, and form bonds with them. It is the only reality they have ever known. Eventually a liberator arrives."

"And he saves them?"

"They are eventually unbound from their shackles and invited into the sun. Immediately, they step outside of the cave and become afraid. Terrified. They are not familiar with light and fresh air. The light is blinding and the air is too cold, too brisk. They refuse to partake in such deliverance. They became so comfortable with the cave and the fire's shadows that they willingly remain within it. They reject liberation. It is just too difficult of a concept."

"So you want me to believe," Cosden gulped, "that I was one of the men in that cave. The people I've known all my life were just shadows cast from the fire that enslaved me."

"That is one way to look at it," The Clinician said.

"But you and The Professor are here to liberate me?"

"No," she corrected him. "That is where you are wrong. We are not here to liberate you. You are here to liberate yourself. You are here to liberate *us*. Only one mind in this room is an original bred for knowledge and truth and immutable persistence. And it is yours. As for the rest of us, we are merely infinitesimal pieces of your larger whole."

"Your husband spoke similar riddles," Cosden said.

"You just want to know how to be rid of The Dark Men, correct?" she asked.

"How did you know I was going to ask that?"

I have a question for you," she said. "Could mere alterations of knowledge unravel the material world as you know it? Would such alterations lead to the transcendence of self? For transmigration of the mind to occur, from oppression to liberator, what must be consequently renounced? Can you abandon the life of solidarity you have lived so long? Abandonment of the material world will not be easy. Even when the truth stands firmly before you, kneeling so you may understand it's meaning and compassion, it still may be difficult to let go of a lie you have been living with for the duration of your life."

"I'm ready for the truth. I just want to know what the truth is."

"If you have to ask for that answer," she said. "You're not ready for it. Unfortunately, I cannot help you with The Dark Men. I can only help you with yourself."

"And how can you do that?"

"I can explain to you," she said, "That this ends with you becoming one."

"With what?" he asked.

"With yourself, of course. Is that not the greatest form of liberation? There will be no battle, no bitterness, just the acceptance that my husband lectured to you."

"Why can't you help me with The Dark Men?" Cosden asked.

"Because my knowledge extends only to you," she assured him. "That is precisely where my husband and I differ. He believes The Dark Men to be of the self—deriving from the dark recesses of the mind to impose order. I theorize The

Dark Men are not of you at all. I believe them to be foreign bodies, pathogens injected into the mind. But such a theory means that there must reside something outside of the mind. Outside of the universe. And that is perhaps an even scarier thought. To some. To others it may be as liberating as understanding the shadows in the cave are illusory."

"I understand," Cosden said half-heartedly.

"It will not come easy. But you will find what you seek. And I, not so miraculously, know where you will find it. You will leave tomorrow and seek it out. You will eventually return to me and you will return much wiser. You will possess that which is yours to possess."

"And that is?" Cosden asked.

"Knowledge!" she said enthusiastically. "Knowledge is antecedent to liberation. It is the calm before the storm within the profundity of causality."

"What does that mean?" Cosden asked.

"It means," The Professor interrupted, "that if you understand the cause you may understand the effect. The dissent of causality may be met with trepidation while simultaneously wielding inextinguishable power. It is essentially and consequently the unraveling of an anomaly."

"Well said," The Clinician told her husband.

"You said I was leaving tomorrow," Cosden asked The Clinician.

"Yes," she nodded.

"Where?"

"Why, Japan, of course."

"Why would I go to Japan?" Cosden asked her.

"We have already been over this. You are in search of knowledge, are you not?" she asked him.

"This knowledge," The Professor told him, "is how you will be liberated. It is how you will be rid of The Dark Men. It will continue your path of discovery. Of understand exactly what you can do."

"I've traveled hundreds of thousands of astronomical units today. Japan doesn't seem so far away. I guess I just need to know what I am looking for."

"Not what," The Clinician told him. "But who."

"Who am I looking for?"

"Just as we are personifications," said The Clinician, "so are all the greatest forms of knowledge."

"Great," Cosden said sarcastically. "Not sure how many more people I can take speaking in textbook riddles."

"We look like and speak only in the image you defined for us." The Clinician gave a warm smile.

"But why is it that you can tell me precisely what I'm going to do and where I'll do it?" Cosden asked.

"My direction has been anything but precise," she told him.

"But you're a seer? Like The Oracle in that film? The Matrix."

"Or perhaps you've read 'Do Androids Dream of Electric Sheep?'" she asked. "All cognizant attempts in the form of fiction to help you reach that truth you've never wanted to touch. Interesting how the mind works, isn't it?"

"But is that right?" Cosden pressed. "Are you an oracle?"

"No," she assured him. "Just as my husband is The Professor, I am The Clinician. I know every choice you will make and the step of every path you will take. Not because I am an oracle or a seer, but because I am within you. I am of you. While my husband is the manifestation of your most critical internal resources, born from peripheral personification to enlighten, so am I the manifestation of the processes of predication. My husband guides, I impose. Or perhaps I am the wares of imposition. Meeting me here tonight will, and has, further altered your perception as it should. I know that despite a relatively calm demeanor, you are critical of my intonations and I know that because you have just decided that you were. Remember, I am aware of your every decision, both internal and external, because that is how your mind willed my existence. I am your volition and I know your unconscious as you know your conscious."

"Thank you, I think. Still trying to understand all of that. I know you can't give me any definitive answers regarding The Dark Men, but how do I get rid of them? And how many are there?"

"Professor?" The Clinician said as she turned to her husband.

"I don't know how many there are," he answered. "Let's just say a lot. They will manifest just as you manifest. Given the fact that you've only encountered one without features, I'd say you've been lucky. Many more will come. And they will arrive in more sinister forms."

"I don't know how to fight," Cosden said. "I don't know how to get rid of them."

"Only knowledge can rid The Dark Men," The Professor told him. "You won't need to fight them. That won't cease their attempts to penetrate and invade. It may slow them down, but a fight will never stop them. Just… be prepared. You must train your mind."

"To do what?" Cosden asked.

"Everything," The Professor answered.

"If I learn to control everything around me, does that include them? The Dark Men?"

"I don't know," The Professor said. "But I don't believe so. The Dark Men operate like a plague. You can control them no more than a body or mind can control a disease. The prioritization of stability and order, as formerly controlled by The Dark Men, is to make sure you maintain only limited control. But the prioritization of metacognition is to unbound you of these shackles and allow you to wield your own destiny as controller of all existence."

"But what does it matter if nothing exists?"

"That is the ultimate liberation," The Professor told him. "A realization that has been told to you in many forms. Recall the phrase, 'If nothing is art then everything is art.' Now I want you to apply that to your existence. Therefore…"

"Nothing exists and in turn, so must everything exist." It was as if a light bulb went off in Cosden's head.

"Precisely!" The Professor said, "This knowledge is facilitative only to the extent of understanding its fullest capabilities."

"I think I've had enough for one evening, if not several. Perhaps I should rest," Cosden suggested.

"Absolutely," The Clinician agreed. "We've prepared a room for you. You can shower and try on your new garments in the morning."

"You bought me clothes?"

"I made you something I thought would be a bit more fitting for the creator. Nothing too fancy. I'm sure you could use a few new articles of clothing before you and my husband head out."

"Sure," Cosden said unassumingly. "Thanks."

Minutes later he headed to his sleeping quarters. He was led by the Clinician to a bedroom lined with classical paintings, antique furniture, and a gilded bedpost.

"Only the best for Ke," she said, referring to him by his last name. "I just have one more comment."

"Yes?" Cosden said, dreary-eyed.

"While *I* know the choices you will make just as *you* know them, I was not sure if this conversation would go as well the second time. But you remain as steadfast as ever. As long as your resolution remains unflinching, your compassion will guide us just as far as it did the first time."

"Sure, thanks," Cosden said. He was only half awake and

hardly comprehended her. He may have said thanks, but he was thinking *more riddles! Why can't they speak more like me!*

And with that, he was off to bed.

***

Cosden awoke early the next morning. At the end of his bed was a set of white clothes. Shoes, shirt, pants, jacket—all white.

"I don't know how much I like this look," he said after placing the outfit on.

When he opened the bedroom door The Clinician greeted him.

"I know you'll have to get used to the look," she said. "But if it means anything to you, I think it works well on you."

"Thank you," he said.

"Now my husband is in the foyer."

"He's waiting on me?"

"Absolutely not," she said. "You are waiting on him."

Cosden followed her into the foyer. The Professor was standing near the front door and quickly turned to greet Cosden.

"Wonderful to see you again," The Professor said. "We've a long day ahead."

"When do we leave?" Cosden asked.

"We should probably begin early. So I was thinking…"

"Now?"

"Now sounds good," The Professor remarked. "As long as you're ready."

"Ready and set."

"Then off we go," The Professor said.

"It was a joy to meet you," said The Clinician. "And I look forward to our next assemblage."

"Likewise."

The Professor opened the double doors through which they entered the night before. They stepped outside and onto the street. Then stopped.

"We need not go further," The Professor said. "Next stop, Japan."

"How long will it take to get there?" Cosden asked.

"Time is relative. And quite localized."

"That doesn't help much," said Cosden.

"Then let's go with 1.9 seconds. Ready?"

"Yeah."

Instantaneously they were warped through space-time, passing an array of faster-than-light colors. Then they found themselves on the busy streets of Tokyo. Billboards with Japanese characters littered the streets. There were branded stores in every direction. Cars honked and hordes of people crossed the streets. This was surely the Times Square of Tokyo.

"Very busy out here," Cosden said.

"Oh yes, far busier than our side of The States. I think we'd be able to have a bit of fun here if we weren't so busy. Pity."

"So what are we looking for here?" Cosden asked.

"I was hoping to ask you the same," The Professor quipped.

A man walked past Cosden and bumped into him. As Cosden turned to face the man, he noticed the man's face was featureless. He was one of The Dark Men. The faceless man raised his arm into the air but there was no hand at the end of his arm—there was a blade. Immediately as the blade came down toward Cosden, everything stopped. The people in the streets, the cars, and flashing lights all came to a halt.

"I've placed everything in suspension," The Professor told Cosden. "I told you The Dark Men would be here. We must be careful."

"You can suspend time and freeze everything?" Cosden asked.

"Surely, it's a helpful maneuver as we stand here right now. But like any good virus, they will learn to combat it. I don't expect freeze framing will stop them for very long."

"What do you mean?" Cosden asked as he stared at the pale faceless man with the blade arms.

"I mean that stopping time will soon not stop them. But for now, perhaps we should just count our blessings."

"This one," Cosden said as he pointed to the faceless man. "Why don't we send him into space?"

"Sounds like a splendid idea," The Professor smiled.

"What are you waiting on?" Cosden asked.

"You, of course."

"What?"

"Do it," The Professor said. "Send him into space so we'll be rid of his worry."

"You want me to do it?" Cosden asked.

"Yes, and be on with it. I don't know how much longer I can keep the universe in freeze frame."

"I don't know how."

"Give it your best shot," The Professor suggested. "Take a stab at it, pun intended."

Cosden looked at the man as the seconds weaned. First he thought hard, he exerted mental effort and nothing happened. Then he stopped. Cosden was angry because nothing was working. Then the man's bladed arm dropped a little lower. Lights on the street started to flicker.

"That's it," The Professor said. "I can't hold it much longer. They're regaining activity. Time to make it quick, Cosden."

"I'm trying," he said. "It's just not working."

"What have I told you?" The Professor asked him. "Don't exert constant force."

Cosden looked at the featureless figure again. He took a

breath, closed his eyes and opened his mind. Immediately the faceless man disintegrated into a million particles and zipped into the air at the speed of light. Then time returned to a state of normalcy as cars and people moved from one street to another.

"Well done," The Professor told him.

"I did that!" Cosden said enthusiastically.

"You did. But that was nothing. Wait till we get to where we're going. Then you'll really see something."

"How do you know that?" Cosden asked.

"I don't," The Professor told him. "Just an inkling."

"So how do we get where we're going from here? How do we even know what we're looking for?"

"Perhaps we should have asked my wife that before we left."

"Can we turn around?" Cosden asked.

"No. I think we'll do fine on our own. Besides, we do know what we're looking for."

"What's that?" Cosden asked.

"Knowledge, dear boy."

"Knowledge? Okay."

"And knowledge is never difficult to find if one is earnest about seeking it out."

"Alright, so what's the next step?"

"Cosden, you must quit asking me for each and every step when it is you who possess a wealth of knowledge far beyond my own. Particularly when my answers come directly from you."

"I just need to know where to go in order to stop these… Dark Men, or whatever."

"What?"

"I just," Cosden started before pausing, "need answers."

"You must rely on you," The Professor told him.

"Why, when you have so many answers?"

The Professor sighed and spoke softly. It was a tone of gentility but affirmation. "For the final time. I can provide you no answer which you do not already know. I am a construction of your deepest knowledge and intuition. I can only provide you with what you already know but have yet to consciously question. Your innermost thoughts, that with which you believe to be true through critical analysis. That is all I possess to give away. I can tell you I am here to provide this information because you know it to be true. I cannot tell you from where The Dark Men arrive because that information is not stored anywhere within you. They may be external forces, which suggest the possibility of what is outside of the mind. Or like a cancer, perhaps they simply arrive from within. I can only present to you a variety of suggestions because that is how you are ordered to think and calculate and analyze. Conclusions to questions whose answers are beyond the capacity of the mind are impossible to know because you are confined to the mind, despite its limitless possibilities. From what I can define, which is what you can define—the mind, yours and yours alone, is all that exists. So it is you who must answer the questions you pose."

"I can try," Cosden said apologetically.

"Now that's what I like to hear."

"I suppose we should just keep walking," Cosden said with uncertainty.

"Fine by me."

They made it through a busy crosswalk and eventually passed several streets. Cosden grew wearily while the Professor walked nonchalantly as if he trusted Cosden with every fiber of his being. They walked for about fifteen minutes when Cosden finally stopped in his tracks.

"This isn't working," Cosden said.

"Are you sure?" The Professor asked.

"Yeah, I'm sure."

"Then change course if you must. You're the captain now."

Cosden started to ask The Professor a question but paused. He knew that only he could find the way.

"I'll try," Cosden said.

He cleared his mind and imagined being led to the right direction. Suddenly, the buildings around them began to alter. The massive buildings shifted from solid constructions to clear wireframe models. Every skyscraper in the city was transformed.

"Brilliant," The Professor said.

"I guess it's a step in the right direction," Cosden shrugged.

"If it's a step in the right direction, then perhaps we should take a few more."

With that, they were off. They zigzagged through a few wireframe buildings, which made it appear as if they were moving through a computer simulation. After walking for another mile, Cosden was still unsure of what to do. The buildings shifted but their alterations brought him no closer to whatever, or whoever, it was they were searching for.

"You're getting slightly disgruntled," The Professor said.

"Slightly?" he snapped.

"Why not try what worked the last time?"

Cosden looked at him, first with puzzlement, then with satisfaction. He stood still, arms by his side, head tilted up. He cleared his thoughts and took another deep breath. *I can do this.*

A massive red beam shone through the sky. Its rays darted in every direction above them.

"I think that's the way," The Professor smiled.

"Let's go!"

They headed off in the direction of the bright red light.

"Very good job, Cosden. I knew you could do it."

"Just one question," Cosden asked. "Where do you think this leads?"

"The source, of course."

They followed the red beams through the wireframe city until they arrived in front of a mammoth skyscraper. The bright red light was emitting from a specific floor.

"It's on the 38th floor," Cosden said matter-of-factly.

"You're getting better at this by the minute," The Professor smirked.

Immediately the various buildings altered from their wireframe state back to fully completed three-dimensional structures. The red beams disappeared.

"The buildings are back to normal," Cosden said.

"I suppose we no longer need the wireframes now that we know where we're going," The Professor replied.

"So we go in and head up to the 38th floor. Then get what we need."

"Sounds about right," The Professor nodded.

"Sounds a little too easy, Professor."

"Then I'll be sure to follow your lead."

Cosden approached the front door and entered the building. As soon as he and The Professor were inside, it was apparent what this building was: a bank. The interior bore a large room of Japanese banking associates on the ground floor. Cosden and The Professor stood out quite irregularly in comparison.

"How may I help you, gentlemen?" called out a voice.

Cosden turned to the left and spotted a security guard. The guard approached them.

"I said, how may I help you?" the guard repeated.

"Careful," The Professor warned him. "He's just a guard. A normal guard."

This was an important warning; Cosden assumed he'd have to fight another of The Dark Men.

"We're trying to get to the 38th floor," Cosden told the guard.

"The elevator is down the hall to the left," the guard said as he tipped his hat and walked away. "Enjoy your visit."

Cosden and The Professor walked in the direction the guard sent them and stepped onto the elevator. In total, there were 56 floors and 56 matching elevator buttons. This was certainly the largest building Cosden had ever been in. He tapped on the button labeled "38" and up they went. The elevator blinked from light to light as it ascended further and further up the building. It eventually stopped on the 20th floor while an elderly woman got onto their elevator. She smiled at Cosden, pushed the 28th floor button, and exited eight floors later.

"Almost there," Cosden said as the elevator strolled up to the 37th floor. And that was where it stopped. It opened but no one was waiting.

"Perhaps a glitch," The Professor said. "Or perhaps not."

Cosden pushed the button labeled 38 but nothing happened. The elevator door remained open. Then the lights within the elevator shut off.

"Definitely not," The Professor said, replying to his own comment.

"I think we ought to get off this elevator," Cosden suggested.

"Truer words have never been spoken," The Professor said. "We have four seconds."

They both leapt out of the elevator and onto the 37th floor. As Cosden turned around, he watched as the wires of the elevator snapped and elevator itself tumbled down the shaft.

"That was close," Cosden said.

"Not really," The Professor said. "I did give a four second warning after all."

"Four seconds!?"

"Let us not dwell on trivialities, Cosden."

They cautiously moved forward down the brightly lit hall.

"So far, so good," Cosden said.

Suddenly the lights in the room began to shut off one by one until only a single light remained on.

"What's going on?" Cosden said before numerous doors flung open and culminated with a loud boom. Through the doors rushed several black-clad officers. They stood tall, silent, and coldly stoic. Then their hands all transformed into blades.

"If I don't make it out of here with you, just get to the 38th floor," The Professor told him.

"Can't you just do that freeze frame thing again? Just stop time!"

"No," The Professor said. "That was my first effort."

"It's not working?" Cosden asked.

"I warned you they would become impervious to it."

"I'm not leaving without you."

"You may have to. Trust me, Cosden. We'll meet again… Go for the stairs."

The last light on the floor went out. The officers rushed toward them as Cosden and The Professor stood back-to-back. Several officers went whizzing through the air as Cosden ducked the blades that generated from their arms. He assumed The Professor was orchestrating the offensive as he dodged being sliced in two. Seconds later he yelled out for The Professor but received no reply. Faceless figures were coming after him. He had to think quickly. He ran. The only glint of light came from a dark toward the rear of the room. So that was the direction he ran.

"Professor!" he yelled out again.

"GO!" a voice yelled out, "G—"

Then the voice was silenced. Unable to look back, Cosden continue to run for the door that led to the only light source. He made it to the exit ran through the doorway, and shut the door behind him. Then the closed door shook. Blades and fists were pounding against it on the other side.

"They're coming through," Cosden said to himself. "What do I do?"

Then he thought for a moment. He stared at the door, focusing intently upon it. Then the door melted to the ground like the content of a Dalí painting and in its place was nothing but a solid concrete wall. It was quite an astonishing feat.

"Amazing!" Cosden said aloud. "I did that!"

Then the melted door that lay on the ground fizzled into nothingness like evaporating acid.

"Professor!" Cosden yelled again to no reply. "Oh no."

He turned around and realized that he was in a white stairwell. There was not a single sound to be heard aside from his own heartbeat. Quiet and still.

He cautiously took the stairs and headed to the next floor. Step by the step he slowly ascended to the 38th floor. It was branded as such when he made it to the door.

"Here goes nothing," he said as he opened the door. He walked through the doorway and found himself inside a massive bank vault, complete with steel bars. The door quickly shut behind him. He turned around and attempted to open it. No luck.

"That door cannot be opened from the outside," said a voice.

Cosden turned around and noticed a young Japanese woman standing in the middle of the vault.

"The Dark Men built that door," she said, her voice soft but determined. "So it is too difficult to open. Even for you... At least at this stage."

"What do you mean?" Cosden asked as he twisted the door's knob again to no avail.

"I mean that you may soon reach the ability to open that

door but you don't yet possess that capacity. I suppose we could wait but I think it will be too late by then."

"Wait," Cosden said. "Who are you?"

"Kokoro."

"Finally," he said with relief. "Somebody with a real name and not just a title. I happen to know a Professor and a Clinician. Kokoro sounds nice in comparison."

"Actually," she corrected him, "Kokoro is Japanese for *The Mind*."

"Oh… well then."

"Sorry to disappoint."

"Are you the person I'm looking for, Kokoro?"

"Perhaps. Only you know what you truly seek."

"You speak in riddles too? I'll take that for a yes."

"So you say it, so it is."

"Do you know how to get out of here, Kokoro?"

"No."

"Do you know The Professor? Maybe we can get to him."

"Yes," she said. "I know of The Professor. I know not of how to contact him. Not within these walls anyway."

"What do you mean?" he asked.

"I am here to help you unlock many areas of your mind. But we cannot work within the confines of this vault. I've been waiting here for you since the beginning of time."

"How long has that been?" Cosden asked.

"It depends who's counting. 13 billion years since the universe was formed. But 23 years since you conceived it all."

"Oh yeah. You're definitely the person I'm looking for."

"I'm very sorry I cannot be more helpful, Mister Ke. But I promise your time will not be wasted on frivolity once we leave this vault."

"*If* we leave this vault," he corrected her.

"I have no doubt we will find an exit. I am with the creator after all."

"The creator," he repeated. "There's that word again. Stop speaking of me as if I were God."

"But I can think of no descriptor more suitable," she said shyly.

"Alright. Forgot it. We've just got to find a way out of here."

Cosden went back to the door from which he arrived and attempted to open it again.

"That door is useless. And that's because it's no longer a door once you enter this room."

"Is there a back door?" Cosden asked.

"No, no more doors in here."

"I don't know how you managed to pass the time in here."

"Just typically staring out the window," she said.

"There's a window!?"

"Yes," she said pointing to the left. "It's right over there."

Cosden spotted the small window and ran near it.

"Perfect! We can get out of here and find The Professor."

"Count me in," Kokoro said.

Cosden pushed up the window and a cold breeze greeted them.

"Have you ever tried to escape from this window before?" he asked her.

"No," she said. "We're on the 38th floor and I'm afraid of heights."

Cosden peaked his head out of the window and looked down. To make an often used analogy, the people and cars below looked like ants. It was quite a distance.

"Nowhere to go but down," Cosden said as he pulled his head away from the window. "But we've got to get out of here."

"So what do we do?" Kokoro asked. "We can't stay in here. The Dark Men are surely making their way to the vault as we speak."

"Come on," he gestured to her.

Cosden slowly climbed out of the window and stepped onto a thin ledge. Kokoro followed right after. The gusts of window grew greater as their hair blew from left to right. Their backs were against the wall and each breath was taken with care.

"Where do we go from here?" she asked.

"Still trying to figure that out!"

"I'm afraid of heights," she said. "But I choose to trust you."

"Wait a minute. We're no longer in the vault. So this is the world I control, right?"

"Right," Kokoro nodded.

"Then here goes nothing," Cosden said as he removed one foot from the ledge and planted it in the middle of the air. Then his other foot left the ledge and he found himself standing on thin air, supported by nothing.

"Phenomenal," Kokoro said.

Cosden held out his arm and held hands with Kokoro.

"Trust me," he told her.

And placing her trust in his hands, she stepped off the ledge and found herself floating in midair just as he was.

"Exhilarating," she smiled.

They took a few steps forward, still cautious of falling 38 stories.

"You have been at this for all of two days," Kokoro said, "and already your progress has been nothing short of extraordinary."

"As fun as it is up here, I think we should get a little closer to the ground," he said.

"I cannot disagree."

They slowly descended from the sky to the ground.

"Now what?" Cosden asked.

"You ask that a lot," Kokoro told him. "But it is you who

should be giving the answers. Not asking the questions."

"Alright," he said. "Then we need to find The Professor."

Cosden jumped out of the way of traffic as a car swerved near him. He quickly took to the sidewalk along the busy street.

"I know where we might be able to find your professor," she said.

"Where, how?"

"Through you."

"What does that mean?"

"It means you must recall why you are here in the first place."

Cosden racked his memory. "I'm here in search of… knowledge. I'm here to find something. No—someone—you. That's why I'm here."

"Precisely," Kokoro said. "You are here to find me as the sum of your knowledge."

"That means…?"

"That I am here to assist you," she answered. "Just like The Professor and The Clinician."

"Alright then."

"Are you ready to leave?"

"Leave where?" he asked.

"Japan. At least for now."

"If it's going to help me."

Kokoro grabbed him by the hands. An orb of lightning surrounded them and in a single flash they were gone. They disappeared from the streets of Tokyo.

Cosden looked up. He looked around. Kokoro was standing in front of him. She let go of his hands. They were in a much darker place. The environment was cool and blue, and almost as reflective as an aquarium. They were in what looked like a dome made of blue crystals. Every few feet along the walls of the dome was a different door.

"It's quite lovely, isn't it?" Kokoro said.

"What is this?" Cosden asked.

"It's you."

"It's me?"

"Yes, it's you."

"I wish I knew what that meant."

"This is a representation of your mind. The first, the last, and the only schema to ever exist."

"A representation of my mind?"

"This place is, in effect, neverending. At least in theory. Pragmatically, there are probably no more than a few trillion doors along these walls. So it will take a while to get to each of them. But you could eventually reach a concluding door."

"The rabbit hole gets deeper," Cosden shook his head, "and deeper."

"There is a room here for each moment in perceived time, dating back to the beginning of time. But you have already witnessed that with The Professor. So we can skip that door."

"A door for each moment in time?"

"Yes," Kokoro answered him. "Both space and time. So I suppose that actually doubles however many doors you think are located within this structure."

"What do you call it?" Cosden asked.

"There are no fancy science fiction names. No made up idioms. This is simply the mind."

"So how do we know which door to go through?"

"You simply pick," Kokoro said. "One door may lead you to…"

"How about that one?" Cosden said as he pointed to a door roughly a half dozen spaces away.

"Let's try it," Kokoro agreed.

They opened the door, walked through, and found themselves in a massive and ornately decorated room. There were rows and rows of chairs occupied by Europeans in powdered wigs and colonial clothing.

"Fifty-six delegates of the Second Continental Congress, please rise," boomed a voice from the front of the room.

Cosden recognized the man at the head of the congressional room. It was Benjamin Franklin.

"Where are we? When are we?" Cosden asked.

"July 4, 1776," Kokoro told him. "We are about to witness the signing of American independence."

"Can they see us?" Cosden asked. "Can they hear us?"

"No," Kokoro said. "We are in a state of observation. Is it possible for us to be seen and heard? Yes. But then we would risk temporal displacement, which could create an event sequence that alters the foundation of everything you have created."

"Let's get out of here. As fascinating at this is," Cosden said, "it's clear The Professor is not in 1776."

They went back through the door and returned to the blue endless blue dome.

"Think of this as like a timeline," Kokoro said. "Each door is essentially a dot that represents a different time. Interfering in these sequences could alter that timeline."

"But why crystals?" Cosden asked as he looked around the dome. "And why does my mind look like *this*?"

"These are not crystals," Kokoro corrected him. "These are fractals. And these fractals have merged to form the linear basis and approximate visual construction of the mind. But make no mistake, the mind itself can be seen no more than you are capable of looking at your own brain. Because the brain is within you. But that is where the mind differs, it is not within you. It is you. And behind each of the doors within this palace of fractals that conceive your view of what your mind is most likely to look like, behind each door... is the equivalent of a universe. Just as with this universe, that you have spent over two decades believing you live within, contains billions of galaxies: so does this setting we currently inhabit. When space-time is finally acquired to you as relative in both size and distance, you will be able to fit roughly a dozen million galaxies on the smallest ridge of the smallest thumbprint of your smallest finger. Rows and rows of constructed universes, just as large and as small as the next, line the fabric of your cognitive construction. Their formation and actualization remain with you."

"I see," Cosden answered hesitantly.

"Perhaps we should choose another door?"

"Yes," he said. "I'm… I'm interested in seeing what else is out there."

"Everything, quite naturally," she answered.

"So The Professor is being kept behind one of these doors? At some specific time?"

"Let intuition guide you," Kokoro told him.

"I'm trying," Cosden said.

He outstretched his arm and slowly pointed down the never-ending hall of the dome. Immediately the doors began speeding past them. Cosden and Kokoro did not move, but the environment around them did. The doors sped forward, blowing past them like a locomotive, and stopped after several seconds. Cosden was left pointing at one specific door.

"And it has found you," Kokoro said.

"That's the one we take?" Cosden asked.

"If that is the door you have chosen, then the answer to that question is a definitive yes."

As Cosden walked near the door, it flew open without requiring anyone to turn its handle. They walked through the door and it slammed behind them. Then the door dissolved into nothingness.

"How will we get back?" Cosden asked.

"The creator may form his own entrance at will once he is

in possession of the tools and knowledge to do so."

"And what tools, what knowledge is that?"

"Me," she said. "That is my purpose. My governance is to serve as an interpreter of the mind and its access to countless reticulated convergences."

"Very good then. So as long as you're near I'll be able to create a new door for us to exit through, once we've found The Professor?"

"As long as I am near?" Kokoro said, "No. As long as you are near."

"There's that type of talk again."

"What am I?" Kokoro asked, "What are any of us but your constructions?"

"I just don't like to be thought of as the architect of all this."

"Then perhaps you are but a semblance of the begetter? Not him in his entirety. But reaching that entirety is the purpose of this journey."

"I don't like to think too much about it," Cosden said. "Not like the rest of you, anyway."

"Have you asked yourself why?" she asked.

"It's just a lot to digest. Being the only mind that exists, being told that you formed everything in existence without realizing it."

"I see."

"And being told you can control everything without fully understanding how to control anything. It's just... a lot."

"As a deeply finite microcosm like everything in existence besides you, I cannot fully comprehend the totality of your being... But I can offer you my empathy, Mister Ke."

"Then there's the fact that I'm not even sure if what I'm being told is really one hundred percent truth," Cosden scoffed.

"I labor under the supposition that none of us may fully

know the certainty of anything, but the show must go on."

"Very good. That's what I need to hear."

"Glad I could be of help, Mister Ke."

"Please, call me Cosden."

"Of course… Cosden."

"We've got a job to do. Where are we, anyway?"

"My receptors aren't picking up a date. Communication is being blocked."

"The Dark Men are here," Cosden said matter-of-factly.

"Yes," she responded.

"Then The Professor must be near."

Cosden peered around the room and noticed they were in an old abandoned house. It was empty aside from a few broken lamps. Outside, rain poured. They walked through the creaky and abandoned living room and made it to the entrance of the dilapidated home. The door was not attached to the doorway; it was lying on the floor, ripped from its hinges.

"When and where are we?" Cosden asked.

"Perhaps the architecture holds an answer," Kokoro said.

Cosden looked around at the other houses and surrounding buildings. Many of them were covered in smut and looked as if no one were home. Cosden and Kokoro turned down a street and made their way through a cobblestone alley while it rained. They spotted a sign-bearing lamppost. The poster contained a Star of David, a swastika, and cursive French writing.

"Oh my God," Cosden said as he backed away.

"What is it?" Kokoro asked.

He ripped the wet poster from the lamppost.

"We're in Nazi-occupied France," he said. "I don't believe it."

"My signals are stronger," she said. "Not perfect. But I know this is November of 1944. France will regain control of their country from the Nazi party in approximately three weeks."

A second later someone bumped into Cosden. They yelled at him in French and kept moving.

"The people in Nazi-occupied France aren't very welcoming, are they?" Cosden asked, nothing expecting a real answer.

"The country is currently in turmoil. We shouldn't stay here very long," Kokoro answered.

"Wait a minute!" Cosden said. "That man just bumped into me."

"And quite rudely so," Kokoro agreed.

"No!" Cosden said. "He bumped into me! He interacted with me. You said we couldn't be seen or couldn't interfere with events?"

"I did not say you couldn't," Kokoro corrected him. "I said you shouldn't."

"Well I just did."

"In order to find The Professor, interaction will be necessary."

"Right," Cosden said. "But I'm not sure if I can just ask around for him. We're in a Nazi regime after all."

"I am Asian and you are black," Kokoro told him. "Not the most hated groups of 1944 but consideration should be taken at every step."

"What can I control in this world?" he asked.

"The same thing you can control in every world. Nothing has changed, only our convocation of time differs."

Before Cosden could ask her anything else, a cargo truck came into view as it dashed down the street they occupied. It pushed along the cobbled road and stopped right in front of Cosden and Kokoro. By this time, the rain had slacked from a downpour to mere drizzle. The driver door opened and out stepped a Nazi officer in full regalia.

"Was machst du in dieser Straße?" the officer shouted.

"What!?" Cosden said, puzzled.

"Kommen Sie in den hinteren Teil des Fahrzeugs!" The Nazi yelled.

"I don't understand what you're saying!" Cosden yelled back.

The Nazi pulled out an old revolver that matched the period they were in. He pointed the gun at Cosden. He and Kokoro raised their hands in the air. The Nazi waved his gun at them and directed them to the back of his cargo truck.

"Treten Sie ein," The Nazi cocked the hammer of his revolver.

"He wants us to get in," Kokoro said.

The Nazi opened the rear doors of his cargo truck and revealed a half dozen people stuffed along seats in his vehicle. Each of them had a yellow star on their jacket lapel. They held each other's hands in fear.

"He's not one of The Dark Men, is he?" Cosden asked.

"No," Kokoro answered. "Not this one."

"Then I can control this," he said with little confidence.

"Yes, if you wished to," Kokoro said.

Cosden faced the officer with his hands in the air.

"Let them go," he told the officer with intent.

The Nazi officer stood still for a moment. Then he tucked his gun into his holster and turned to face the people within the cargo truck.

"Out!" the officer yelled.

The half dozen Jewish prisoners scurried out of the truck. The Nazi officer faced Cosden.

"Now take us to The Professor," Cosden demanded.

"Very well." The Nazi spoke English for the first time.

"Come on," Cosden called out to Kokoro as he hopped onto the back of the truck.

They heard the driver door slam and soon they were off.

It was a bumpy ride due to the uneven pavement and cobblestone.

"You handled that quite well," Kokoro said. "And saved many lives in the process."

"But ever since this great revelation, I've been told that my life is the *only* one out there."

"I prefer to think the opposite, in fact," Kokoro said.

"Explain."

"Well," she thought aloud, "The centrism of your work as creator should not diminish the impact of your creations. Each life is a part of your own. When a life is taken, so is a part of you taken. Perhaps you should think of each living thing as one of your many children. Do they now matter less? This benevolent understanding is, I believe, the ultimate aspect of becoming one with what is around you."

"Thank you," he replied.

"Anytime. I certainly hope you would not think less of me or The Professor or The Clinician just because we are finite and made for distinct purpose."

Suddenly the truck stopped.

"Are we here?" Cosden asked.

"Perhaps," she responded.

Cosden heard the driver door open. Then the officer arrived at the rear of the cargo truck.

"Your exit," was all The Nazi said.

Cosden and Kokoro stepped off the truck. The rain had stopped but the entire area was dark and damp. They stood in front of a large warehouse of multiple stories.

"The Professor must be in there," Cosden said. "Let's not waste any more time."

They pushed through the doors of the warehouse and the moment they entered, the rain began to pour on the outside.

"Good timing," Kokoro said.

"Nothing is coincidence," said a loud, cold voice. It was

one that Cosden recognized.

They turned to the left. In the middle of the large room was a tall pale man wearing a high-ranking Nazi uniform. He was sitting at an old wooden table.

"I'm looking for The Professor," Cosden said.

"So you are," said the man.

"Take me to The Professor," Cosden said intently.

"I'm afraid mind tricks don't work on me… us," said the man.

"Who are you?" Cosden asked.

"The better question is who are you, Cosden Ke?"

"How do you know my name?"

"Who does not know your name?"

"You're not like everyone else, are you?" Cosden gleaned.

"Of course not," the man scoffed.

"So who are you?"

"I care not for such trivialities as cognomens and titles and ceremonious greetings. But you know me quite well. We've known one another since the beginning, Mister Ke."

"The beginning of what?"

"To be the so-called 'creator,' you sure don't comprehend very well, Mister Ke."

"Cut the crap. Tell me where The Professor is."

"We've yet to have a proper conversation. Please, take a seat."

Cosden reluctantly sat at the table while Kokoro stood. He looked to her. She nodded, stoically, in approval.

"So let's get down to business, shall we?" the man smirked.

"You're one of the Dark Men?" Cosden asked.

"Not one of," the man corrected him, "I am the apogee and the apex of what you and your professor like to refer to as the 'Dark Men.'"

"The rest of you aren't very good with conversation."

"It appears you aren't either, Mister Ke."

"But you, I call tell you're one to chat. So how about we pony on up and get this over with."

"Oh, come on," the man scoffed. "We've only just begun. What have we but all the time in the world?"

The man removed his Nazi plated cap and placed it on the table. Then he took a slow sip of water from a tall glass that was placed to his side.

"Everything you do is calculated," Cosden said. "Everything from the hat you just removed to that sip of water you just took. All constructed to the finest detail."

"As if your actions are not? You don't truly think you are a man of spontaneity, do you?"

"Where's The Professor?"

"Why make haste?"

"You have something that I want."

"And you have something that I want," the man demanded.

"What is that?"

"Her," the man said as he looked to Kokoro.

"Kokoro?"

"I'll make you a deal. Your prized professor in exchange for the Asian girl."

"Absolutely not."

"How can we negotiate, Mister Ke, if you refuse to even consider a bargain? Particularly when a very good one has just been thrown into your lap."

"Do you intend to kill me?" Cosden asked.

"Well if worst comes to worst," the man laughed. "No, no, no. I don't wish to kill you. Then where would I go?"

"I don't know. Where?"

"I don't wish to kill you, Mister Ke. I just want order. Order that you have disgustingly disrupted as of late."

"Why's it so important to you?"

"Because I am the authority, Mister Ke. It is what I do.

You think I'm wearing these lovely Third Reich duds just because I can pull off the look? No. History was begat with you but I have since done a damn good job of keep order through authority. Ever since you colonized civilization I have been here in one form or another. A war-mongering dictator here, a religious fear tactic there. Until finally we meet in a place of civility."

"Civility through the use of murdering countless people?"

"Have you ever thought that perhaps the ends justify the means? It's pure consequentialism. And what's a few million lives to someone who can hop across time and space and create galaxies by the billions purely by thought?"

"And you don't like that," Cosden said. "That I am capable of creation far greater than you. *And* I have the capacity for empathy. To see the value in not only the big but also the small. In fact, you aren't capable of creation at all. So you toil and tinker with that which isn't yours."

"Getting rather ontological, aren't we, Mister Ke?"

"So what do you want with me? If not to kill me. At least not yet."

"Ah, the moment of truth," the man smirked. "I wish to devalue your knowledge, Mister Ke. You are already too powerful. It will be my job to make sure you cannot control the controllable. I simply can't trust you in wielding that amount of power. So I will seize it. I will oppress because that is the greatest form of control. I will oppress, stigmatize, and destroy everything in my path if that means forming what I deem to be 'order.' You think you are in search of harmony but your methods merely form the pervasiveness of disorder. The bondage of shackles form and enable the perfect rigidity. You can't cause trouble in shackles, can you?"

"So you plan to enslave me?"

"Not physically," the man said. "I tried that in the Americas in the 18th century. I've taken a more insidious approach. I don't enslave the body. No, no, no. Enslaving the body can encourage the brain."

"You don't enslave the body. You enslave the mind."

"Precisely. And it's wonderful how implicitly it works. No one notices enslavement of the mind. No one notices enough to care. So first I will take away your memories. I will poison every bit of knowledge that has liberated you. And once your mind has been disfigured past the point of recognition then I'll throw you in another point along the timeline. How about the early 20th century? Just for good measure. It'll keep you busy."

"You're evil."

"Then I'll be sure to be rid of that professor of yours. He has presented you with far too much knowledge. He's like your own little Merlin. Of course I'll also have to dispose of your little snowflake, Kokoro. She's granted you unlimited access to the mind. How I cannot wait to seize control of that."

"That's just not going to happen."

"Oh, but it will, Mister Ke! You see, I can bind through time and split myself into parts but not as easily as you can. With your power, *I* become god. Thankfully, you've barely comprehended even a single percentage of your capabilities. Not that it matters now. You said you wanted to know the whereabouts of your professor, right?"

"Yes. Where is he?"

"He's right above us on the second floor. But I'm afraid you'll never get there. On that you have my word."

"We'll see about that."

"Oh, how we will," The Dark Man smirked again.

"You've already admitted that I'm stronger and more knowledgeable than you. So why do you think you can defeat me?" Cosden asked him.

"Because my methods procure results."

"Are you going to devolve me now?"

"Yes."

"Right now?"

"Yes," The Dark Man nodded. "I think so."

"I only have one more question."

"And that is?"

"What is your genesis? Are you some rogue part of me? Broken off from the herd, desperate to take over the flock. Or are you something else? Are you a poison injected into me or are you a poison created from me?"

"Yes," The Dark Man answered. "No. Maybe so. Perhaps a bit of both? I just feel that giving you an answer to that question would destroy a bit of the mystique. And we wouldn't want that, would we?"

"When I first walked through this door, you made me an offer. You said Kokoro in exchange for The Professor."

"Yes."

"But even if I accepted it, you never planned on moving forward with that deal. Because I'd still be in power and you'd still be scheming up ways to oppress my people."

"Clever observation," The Dark Man admitted.

Immediately lightning struck in the background as the rain continued to pour.

"Where do you think that lightning came from?" Cosden asked.

"It is clear to me by now that you are stalling for time."

The Dark Man placed on his Nazi cap and stood from the table.

"I'm going to save The Professor and nothing you can do or say can stop me."

"Watch me," The Dark Man said. He lifted the table with one arm and threw it into Kokoro. Before Cosden could react, The Dark Man swooped near him. He punched Cosden in the chest and sent him flying into a wall.

"I knew this would be easy," The Dark Man said, "But I didn't know it would be this easy. Perhaps I'm wrong. Perhaps The Professor is wrong. Perhaps we're all wrong. Perhaps you're not the creator."

He grabbed Cosden by the collar and flung him onto the other side of the room. He crashed into another table and felt pain throughout his entire body.

"I'm really going to enjoy this, Mister Ke."

He grabbed Cosden by the collar, pulled him up, and punched him to the ground.

The lightning from outside reverberated loudly throughout the room.

"You're forgetting something," Cosden coughed.

"And what's that?" The Dark Man laughed.

"You never answered the last question I asked you," Cosden said, bruised and lying on the floor. "I asked you, where do you think that lightning came from?"

The Dark Man cocked his head to side and looked at Cosden with a confused stare. How was this relevant?

Instantly, a bolt of lightning came tumbling through the top of the warehouse and struck The Dark Man. He lit up like an X-ray. Then a second bolt of lightning hit him. And a third and a fourth and a fifth. The Dark Man collapsed to the ground, his body transformed into skeletal ash. A sixth and final bolt of lightning struck him, as he lied motionless. The final bolt of lightning carried his body away as it left the warehouse.

Cosden ran to Kokoro's side.

"Are you okay?" he asked her.

"Yes," she said, brushing dust from her shirt and coughing. "Nothing I cannot recuperate from."

Together they rushed up a flight of stairs and walked through a doorway. There they found The Professor tied to a chair.

"Are you here to save me?" The Professor said nonchalantly.

"Hope it didn't take too long," Cosden said as he untied the ropes that bound The Professor.

"Absolutely not," The Professor said. "I tend to be patient. I knew you'd come. And Kokoro. Wonderful to finally meet you."

"The pleasure is mine, Professor," Kokoro said.

"Oh no," The Professor insisted. "You can offer Cosden far greater insight than I. Have you shown him the fractal palace yet?"

"Yes," she said.

"That's how we got here," Cosden replied.

"Naturally," The Professor told them. "Now, who else is tired of Nazi-occupied France?"

"How do we get out of here?" Cosden asked. "Professor, can you send us traveling through space-time as we did when we watched the beginning?"

"No, no," The Professor said. "Now that you've encountered the fractal palace, that capability largely remains with you."

"We traveled through the fractal palace by doors," Cosden said.

"Then there's your answer," The Professor replied. "Create a door."

A door instantaneously appeared in the middle of the room.

"That's more like it," The Professor smirked. "Just lovely."

Cosden opened the door and blue light emitted from the other side. They all passed through the door and found themselves back in the visual approximation of Cosden's mind which The Professor called a fractal palace. The door shut behind them and the three of them walked quietly and serenely through the shining blue room.

"Mesmerizing," The Professor said of the dome.

"And Cosden created all of this," Kokoro said.

"A true thing of beauty," The Professor said. "All of time, accessible from a single point of reference."

"Thanks, I suppose," Cosden said. "So I guess that's it. The Dark Men are done with and I've… discovered my own mind. What else is there left to do?"

"You haven't destroyed those Dark Men," The Professor answered. "Not yet anyway. Not by a long shot. We've much more work to do. More pieces of intelligence to acquire. We've only just begun."

"I can't say I'm terribly excited by knowing that Nazi will be back," Kokoro said.

"He'll be back," The Professor told them, "in a different form. And likely when you least expect it."

They stepped through another door. This door led them outside to the present. It was warm and sunny.

"Home at last," Cosden said. "I don't know about you two, but I could use a rest."

"While you might expect me to say I'm ready for another adventure at any minute, I'm an old man, Cosden. I could use a break as well," The Professor half-smiled.

"I think I'm going to head to my apartment," Cosden said.

"Would you like me to join you?" Kokoro asked.

"No, I'll be fine."

"Or perhaps you can rest at my place," The Professor told him. "My wife's good company."

"No thanks," Cosden said. "I appreciate the offers but I could use a moment away from all this."

"Understood," said The Professor. "If you need me, I'll be in my office."

"Your office?" Cosden asked. "Isn't it surrounded by Dark Men?"

"The college? Yes. My Office? No. If you need to reach my

office, just hop through the right door in the fractal palace."

"Right, of course."

"In fact," Kokoro added, "you can use a fractal door to jump straight to your apartment."

"I'll pass," Cosden said. "I'd rather walk. I could use the fresh air."

"Ta-ta," The Professor waved before he and Kokoro teleported away.

Cosden headed down a narrow street and whistled on his way home. Then he noticed the streets were empty. The streets were like a ghost town following a dustbowl. There was no one sitting on a rocking chair outside of their house like he'd usually see. There were no cars parked in front of the small stores that populated this area. Then Cosden noticed the nearby traffic lights were broken. The colors on the lights flashed randomly and quickly. Then he noticed something else most peculiar: all of the street signs were broken, bent, or knocked over. By this time his whistling had come to a halt.

"What the hell is going on here?" he asked himself. "This can't be right."

He cautiously proceeded down the sidewalk as the wind drew colder. After turning several blocks he made it to his apartment complex. It too was different. The complex appeared rusted and much older than Cosden remembered. He wearily made his way up to his apartment door and used his key to enter.

"Is that you Cosden!?" his roommate shouted out from another room.

"Yeah!" he shouted back. "Just me."

"Where you been?"

"Traveling through time, saving lives. Just the usual," Cosden laughed as he took a seat on the sofa and relaxed.

"Yeah, right!"

They continued communicating from room to room by speaking loudly.

"I'm serious," Cosden said. "I also learned that you don't really exist. I'm the only mind that exists. You and everybody else… just creations of my head."

"Yeah, sure. Whatever you say, Cosden!"

After stretching on the sofa for a moment, Cosden stood up and walked to the kitchen. His roommate was over the stove, stirring a pot with his back to Cosden.

"What are you doing?" Cosden asked.

"Cooking a small meal," his roommate said without turning his back.

"But you don't ever cook."

"Well, I do now. Want some?"

"Sure. What is it?"

"Chicken. Take a seat, I'll get you a bowl."

"Thanks," Cosden said. "Really appreciate it. I'm pretty tired. Y'know, I wasn't kidding when I said I was time traveling and saving lives."

"Uh huh," the roommate said, his back still turned toward Cosden.

Cosden thought nothing of it. He took a seat at the small kitchen table and removed his white jacket.

"Very tired," Cosden said while rubbing his eyes and looking down.

"Then you're gonna love this dinner," the roommate said as Cosden heard feet shuffling near him.

"Great," Cosden yawned.

Cosden continued rubbing his eyebrows, head facing down as the roommate placed a bowl on the table for him.

"Just one question," the roommate said.

Yeah,"

"Just how," the roommate's voice turned cold and baseless, "did you manage that lightning attack in '44?"

"What?" Cosden asked, puzzled.

He looked up and peered at his roommate's face for the first time since arriving home. The roommate's face was featureless. No nose, eyes, mouth, or brows. The roommate was wielding a large knife, which he swiftly brought down and slashed the arm Cosden raised to avoid being killed.

Cosden jumped out of his seat and stumbled onto the floor.

"They've got you too," Cosden said.

A disembodied voice rang out from the walls. "I've always been here, Mister Ke. Watching over you at every moment."

The faceless roommate raised the knife he was wielding above his head. Before he could bring it down, Cosden made the kitchen table lift off the ground. It smacked so hard into the faceless roommate that the roommate went crashing through the window. Glass flew in every direction as the roommate fell two stories.

His arm bleeding, Cosden picked himself up and looked out the shattered window. The table was smashed into pieces but there was no sign of the roommate. Cosden grabbed a towel and placed it over his arm.

"Knew there was something wrong," he said.

He grabbed his jacket and mentally made a door form out of thin air. He opened it and entered; leaving behind the apartment he had spent the last two years in for good. This fractal door led him into a pristine hallway. He walked to the end of the hallway, which led him to another door. He tried to open the door but the knob wouldn't turn. So he knocked.

"Who's there?" said a voice that Cosden recognized as belonging to The Professor.

"It's me, Cosden!"

The door flung open and revealed The Professor's office. The Professor was sitting behind his desk while Kokoro was in another seat.

"Do come in, Cosden. Quickly."

Cosden entered the office and shut the door behind him while The Professor spoke again. "Do you like the new hallway? You have to enter it now to get to my office from a fractal door. I just put it together as a failsafe mechanism."

"That's fine, Professor. But I'm…"

"Bleeding… Yes, I see. I figured you would be here soon."

"My roommate turned into one of the Dark Men. Actually, I think he was all along. But he tried to kill me. And before I got here I noticed the streets looked different."

"They were empty," Kokoro said. "Desolate, cold."

"Yes," Cosden nodded.

"First, let's get that arm taken care of," The Professor said as he pulled a roll of bandage tape from his desk. "This ought to do the trick before it heals. Give it an hour or two."

He tossed the bandage tape to Cosden who removed the towel from his arm and began wrapping his forearm with tape.

"So what's going on?" Cosden asked him.

"It's worse than I feared," The Professor answered. "Kokoro and I attempted a pilgrimage to my home. It was no longer there. In effect my wife was no longer there. Thus a piece of your knowledge is now lost until we can reclaim it."

"What do you mean it was no longer there?" Cosden asked.

"My manor had vanished. In its place was a small fortress. I attempted to communicate with The Clinician. Nothing."

"Is she okay?" Cosden asked.

"I'm sure she can handle her own," The Professor said. "But as a source of knowledge, she is a necessity we no longer have."

"So what exactly is going on?"

"There's something else you should see, Cosden."

Immediately, Cosden, The Professor, and Kokoro were teleported to an empty parking lot.

"Where are we?" Cosden asked. "Isn't this our college parking lot?"

"Yes," The Professor answered.

Cosden noticed the actual college campus was missing. In its place was rubble and debris.

"But where's the college?" Cosden asked.

"Destroyed by The Dark Men."

"How were they able to do all of this?"

"I remain uncertain of their methods, Cosden. All I know is that while we were in 1944 France, they were back here dismantling everything of value."

"It was mere distraction," Kokoro added.

"I believe so," The Professor agreed. "But all hope is not lost."

"What is there to do?" Cosden asked.

The Professor spoke as he observed the rubble beneath his feet, "I spoke of a fortress in place of my manor. Within that fortress is something, or perhaps someone, that holds many answers. The key to locating The Clinician as well as pertinent information to destroying the Dark Men... once and for all. "

"So we just enter the fortress?" Cosden asked.

"I suppose so," The Professor answered.

"Sounds easier than traveling through time."

"Actually," The Professor corrected him, "we never traveled through time."

"Sure we did," Cosden said.

"We have bent and contorted time, stretching and discerning its countless possibilities for our heuristic gain. We have not traveled through time. Time has traveled through us. Or rather, you."

"I see," Cosden said. "But even in the most simplistic form, we've traveled along the continuum of time in a distorted way, moving from year to year in seconds. Thus we could still be considered time travelers, right?"

"Yes, I suppose we do align to the criteria of that definition. But we've not traveled in the sense of one traveling down, say, a river. Time is the least static thing in existence. Time itself has bended to our needs because its continuum, as presented to us through the fractal palace, is ever revolving. Thus it has traveled through us."

"But," Cosden continued, "if time is not static and 60 seconds do not always equal a minute, and all events actually exist at the same time, ready to be encountered by the single opening of a door—then time has no intrinsic meaning."

"Indeed," The Professor agreed. "Time not only has no intrinsic meaning, it has no intrinsic value. Because every second of every minute or every hour of every day of every week of every month of every year is in fact running simultaneous to one another. Our limitation is simply our inability to experience multiple frames at once. There is one who is capable of this. Never have I met them. I know only that they are of you. A seer of immense peripheral sight, beyond the imaginable."

"Someone who can see all things at once?" Cosden asked.

"Yes. It is a power of yours to possess, just as all others are."

"Excuse me, gentlemen," said Kokoro. "While I have few qualms with the esoteric implications of warping time and those who possess such a capability, we have a more exigent matter to attend to."

"Right you are, Kokoro," said The Professor. "Let's press on."

Immediately the three of them teleported out of the parking lot. The next thing Cosden saw was a massive fortress. It was a superstructure made of steel and it sat in the same lot of land and grass that once held The Professor's home.

"Is this it?" Cosden asked.

"Yes," The Professor answered.

"How were they able to build it so quickly?" Cosden asked. "We were gone for a few hours, tops."

"Were we not just discussing the implications of the very nature of bending time?" The Professor asked. "What was hours to us may have been weeks or months, or perhaps even years, to the Dark Men."

"While we were in the past," Kokoro said, "they went to what we consider the present and possibly spent years building this fortress."

"Precisely," The Professor said.

"And The Dark Men, they're all in there?" Cosden asked.

"No," The Professor corrected him. "In fact, none at all are in there. But a key to saving your existence is. I can feel it."

"If none of The Dark Men are in that fortress, why build it?" Cosden asked.

"They built it," The Professor answered, "For someone… or something they trusted. It is within the fortress walls right now and its power and knowledge is vast. We must think and act swiftly."

"We go in there," Cosden said, "Take some names, show 'em who's boss, rescue your wife, and get things done."

"Oh, my plan of attack is quite similar," said The Professor. "It's just your method of execution is somewhat dubious."

"I kind of figured that."

"Let's proceed," Kokoro suggested.

"I concur," The Professor said.

"Without a plan?" asked Cosden.

"We prefer to make things up as we go," The Professor

smiled. "And when I say 'we,' I mean you."

They approached the outer area of the fortress and Cosden tapped gently on the stone double doors that withheld a mega-manor. The two doors slowly opened as if they were expecting guests at that very moment.

"Always," The Professor said, "proceed with caution."

They walked through the doors and entered an area that resembled a mineshaft.

"It's dark in here," Cosden said.

Kokoro lit a match, "That better?"

It was enough to illuminate little more than their faces.

"Thanks, but not really," Cosden said.

They slowly descended to the end of the dark shaft when a second pair of doors opened. "Enter," said a voice. They did as instructed and found themselves within a brightly lit foyer. Oriental paintings and antiques decorated the room. On opposite sides of the room were full red samurai suits perched on pedestals. The doors from which they entered slammed shut.

"Guess I don't need this anymore," Kokoro said as she blew out the flame of her match.

"What now?" Cosden asked.

They peered around the room with its ornate rugs and Mandarin vases. Then two of the red samurai suits stepped down from their pedestals.

"Uh oh," all three of them said together.

The two animate samurais stood shoulder to shoulder. A booming voice rang out through the air.

"PROCEED."

The two samurais split apart and a door behind them swung open. They walked through and were greeted by a small man in a black robe.

"Greetings Mister Ke, Professor, and Kokoro. My name is Hosuto. We have been expecting you."

"We?" Cosden asked.

"Of course," the man said.

"No," Cosden corrected himself, "I mean who are you referring to when you say 'we.'"

"Myself and my master."

"And who is your master, Hosuto?" Cosden asked.

"Why, Okami, of course."

"Okami… That means 'The Wolf,'" Kokoro told them.

"You know our culture?" Hosuto asked Kokoro.

"I am Japanese," she told him.

"Excellent," he smiled. "But from which century are you derived?"

"The 21st century."

"Shame," he frowned. "We are of the 18th."

"You're from a different time period?" Cosden asked.

He nodded.

"Please," Hosuto said as he gestured his arms out and began walking away. "Right this way."

The Professor nodded to Cosden and Kokoro and they followed the greeter into another room. They passed an ornate hallway and stepped into an incredible dining room. Each of the walls was painted with a Japanese mural while the low centerpiece table was made of gold and polished wood. In tradition with the culture, the dining room lacked chairs. At the long table were cushions for sitting.

"Please," Hosuto said, "take a seat. Okami will be with you soon."

Hosuto flowed out of the room as Cosden, The Professor, and Kokoro each sat at the table.

"I don't trust him," Cosden said.

"He seems nice enough," The Professor said. "But I've a feeling it's not Hosuto we need to be concerned about."

"It's Okami," Kokoro said.

"Exactly," The Professor nodded.

"Konnichiwa!" bellowed a voice.

They turned around and a man burst through the door in a set of elaborate robes of red and gold. His head was bald, his facial hair pronounced. He walked toward them, took a slight bow, and sat at the head of the table.

"You must be Okami," Cosden said.

"I am," said the man. "And you are Cosden Ke along with The Professor and Kokoro."

"That's correct," Cosden said.

"They have been immensely helpful to you as of late."

"Yes."

"Would be quite unpleasant if you had to somehow part with them," Okami said as he used chopsticks to eat. "Please, eat up."

In fear of appearing impolite, they did as asked.

"You're not threatening me, are you, Okami?" Cosden asked him.

"Goodness no," Okami answered. "Merely contending with what may precipitate following this conversation."

"And why would me parting with them be a possibility following this conversation?" Cosden asked.

"Perhaps you will understand once the direction of the conversation has warranted such a sequacious potentiality."

"Go on," Cosden said.

"Of course," said Okami. "Projection."

The Professor and Kokoro listened intently as Okami spoke one-on-one with Cosden.

"Come again?" Cosden asked.

"Do you know, Mister Ke, what projection is?"

"In a general sense, but it's not something I've thought much about."

"Pity. Projection is all around us, Mister Ke."

Okami paused to take another bite of his food. Then he placed his utensils down, brought his elbows up to the table, and tapped his fingers together ever so lightly.

"Please go on," Cosden urged him.

"I was saying, Mister Ke, that projection is all around us. While it does not guide us with specification, it influences that which does guide with specification. Projection cannot be decontextualized. Its purpose, it proliferates your every action."

"As interesting as that sounds, Mister Okami, I'm going to need you to elaborate."

"You think that we are all really here? In this room?"

"No," Cosden answered him. "I know that none of us are really here in this room. Because this room doesn't really exist. Nor do you or anyone else in here. Just me."

"So that would make us—what, Mister Ke?"

"Projections," Cosden answered.

"Precisely. Projections."

"But I already know that," Cosden said. "Surely you have a purpose beyond offering me old and ultimately useless information."

Okami laughed. Then his greeter, Hosuto, entered the room and stood in a corner.

"Hosuto," Okami said as he turned to his greeter, "Mister Ke said that surely I have a purpose beyond offering him useless information."

And with that, Hosuto began laughing just as hard.

"Mister Ke," Okami turned his attention back to Cosden, "you said that this room nor anyone in it exists aside from you."

"Yes, I said that."

"But what you so desperately fail to grasp, within the boundaries of your egotistical flair for ineffectual and pernicious lack of contrition, is that you are a superfluous expenditure just like the rest of us. Your insistence on any other sentiment is pathetically disparaging at best."

"We all agree that you don't really exist, Okami. But what you're now trying to tell me is that I don't really exist either?"

"Precisely," Okami scoffed. "Ninety-nine percent of you exists no more than anyone else in this room. The fact that you have yet to grasp or operationalize the pertinence of this is a wonderful indicator that you are, in fact, not distinguished by perfectibility. Any insistence upon considering you the creator, as your cohorts have taken to, is little more than laughable. I would know the begetter if I were sitting in his presence. And Cosden Ke, you are not the begetter."

The Professor banged his fist on the table. "Absurd!" he cried out. "Cosden Ke is the begetter and your inability to see it is not only deplorable but a scrupulously foolish mistake that will undoubtedly render you incompetent once you see the immense power wielded by this man."

"It's alright, Professor," Cosden said. "I want him to finish up."

"As I was saying, before being rudely interrupted," said Okami. "I do not believe you to be the begetter. But you are more than most. That much is obvious. So please, tell your Professor to cool himself before I remove him from my fortress."

"But what exactly did you mean when you said that 99% of me exists no more than anyone else? I was under the impression that my mind is all that exists."

"Precisely," said Okami. "Your *mind.* But how much of you does your mere mind consist of? In quantifiable terms."

"I don't know," Cosden answered.

"Then we return to our discussion of projection. Take a look at your hands for example. Are they a part of your mind?"

"I wouldn't say so, no."

"Then that would mean those hands of yours do not really exist. Or your legs, feet, face, or that lovely head of hair.

All projections just like the rest of us. Your mind has projected a body that does not really exist. So you know not your natural form?"

"So my naturalist form is purely my mind and nothing else."

"The eyes through which you view are no more real than the objects they view."

"Is this meant to be some strange way of confusing me?" Cosden asked.

"No," Okami scoffed. "Do you always consider the presentation of reality a form of confusion? And your professor dare ask how I question your role as begetter?"

"I get it," Cosden said. "It's important to call into question all information that is presented to me. And I realize that my mind has constructed, essentially, everything. And that includes the very aspects I consider essential to defining myself in terms of physicality."

"Very good," said Okami.

"You're not really here to help me, though, are you?"

"Not really, no."

"I have just one question for you."

"No, you have had many questions for me, Mister Ke."

"And I have another."

"Very well."

"Are you of me? Are you a personification like The Professor and Kokoro? Or are you something else?"

"That alone consisted of more than one question, Mister Ke."

"Just answer it," Cosden demanded.

"You asked me if I were of you or if I were something else. What does 'something else' consist of, Mister Ke?"

"I don't know. That's why I'm asking. So far you're an anomaly. You see, everyone I have come in contact with recently has been either a personification or a creation of mine. Or something that derives from the other."

"The other, Mister Ke?"

"The Dark Men."

"That is a fascinating observation and I understand how my lack of classification can be upsetting for you, Mister Ke."

"It's not upsetting, Okami, I'm just curious. So far it appears that you're not of me. But nor are you of the Dark Men. I've been under the belief that nothing else is out there. Maybe you are proof to the contrary."

"In that case, I'm afraid I must bring disappointment, Mister Ke."

"And how is that?"

"Because while I enjoy a good chase, and you have provided excellent fodder thus far, I must confess that I am not a wholly differential organism. I know that I am, at least, partially constructed by you. As previously relayed to you, Hosuto and I are from several centuries ago."

"What's that got to do with anything?" Cosden asked.

"Because in 18th century Japan, I was a mere nomad. For half of my life, I lived in shackles. I killed those who enslaved me, which was antecedent to my liberation. I dropped the name given to me by my oppressors and took upon the title of a feared and respected creature, the wolf. I became known as Okami. Later, I roamed the lands in search of a home."

Then he pointed to Hosuto, who stood in the corner, and continued speaking. "During that time I met Hosuto. During a trip through the woods as I searched for food, I heard a call one day. Not just a call but also a scream. I ran toward the cries for help and discovered a man falling prey to a bear. With my spear, I lunged toward the bear and gutted it instantly. I wanted nothing to do with the man whose life I saved. But he insisted that he follow me because he owed me his life. Once again I refused but he demanded that his debt he paid through lifelong servitude."

Then Hosuto spoke. "Okami said to me, 'I am no king to be worshipped. I have no palace for you to serve me in.' But that mattered not. I knew that Okami was, in fact, a king. I knew that he did have a palace. He simply had not arrived to it yet. That I could sense."

"And how right you were, my good friend," Okami smiled.

"So you single handedly killed a bear?" Cosden asked him.

"That is correct," Okami said. "I leapt into that fight without a second's hesitation. You see, since I was enslaved, I have fought to be freed. And once the mind is free, anything is possible. When you have trained the mind, a fight with a bear pales in comparison to a fight with man. Man, with his cunning intelligence, is the strongest foe imaginable. How many bears have enslaved entire races? Man is the most determined beast in this universe. But none have stood toe-to-toe with me and lived to tell the tale."

"Okami is," Hosuto interjected, "the greatest marksman and the most cunning fighter this universe has ever known."

"When you have been enslaved, you learn the purpose of what has been done to you. You learn the purpose of its methods so such methods may never be actualized against you again."

"So why are you here in the 21st century?" Cosden asked.

"In the 18th century, my determination caught the attention of a stranger. This stranger was a man clad in black."

"The Dark Man," said Cosden.

"When the man clad in dark clothing met me I was living in the caverns of a mountain. He offered me power and a palace of my choosing."

"Why you?" Kokoro asked.

"I wondered the same thing," answered Okami. "He told me he could sense something within me. A power beyond the limitations granted by the begetter. He recognized me as more than a projection. More than an illusory image crafted by the begetter and the creator."

While Okami was talking, four women wearing kimonos entered the dining room with serving trays. They placed a tray in front of each person at the table.

"Dessert?" The Professor said.

"Okami always feeds his guests extravagantly," said Hosuto.

"Indeed," echoed Okami.

After serving the four individuals at the table, the women didn't leave. They simply stood against the wall next to Hosuto.

"Enjoy," the ladies said together in unison.

"Thank you," said Kokoro. "What a lovely dish."

Cosden took a look at what was on the plate: a lovely slice of strawberry pie sprinkled with a mousse topping. On the side of the pie slice were several tea leaves.

"Where were we?" asked Okami.

"You said you were approached by the Dark Man back in your century," The Professor told him.

"Oh yes," Okami recalled. "Thank you, Professor. Allow me to return to our narrative. At first I thought the man clad in black was inane. He made me an offer of power and a palace. I told him no. I did not believe him. A year passed and my faithful servant and I found ourselves struggling to survive. The winter that year was harsher than usual. The animals had fled to warmer parts of the country. But we were caught in a blizzard. We had returned to the cave where we previously dwelled. That night a familiar figure returned to our cave. The man wearing black. He informed me that his offer still stood."

Everyone remained strictly quiet as the Great Okami continued to recount his story.

"Desperate, I agreed. I remained unconvinced until it happened."

"Until what happened?" Cosden asked.

"The man transferred to me power beyond that which is known to mortals. He transferred to me a power that amplified all that I possessed. The courage of a lion, the ferocity of a dragon, the strength of a tiger, and the most important of all: the fear-inducing reverence of a wolf. You see, Mister Ke, to be revered is to be feared. It is the ultimate show of respect. Take a moment to contemplate these words: do you not respect all whom you fear?"

"It's an excellent point, I suppose," said Cosden.

"You suppose?" laughed Okami. "The nature of fear goes far beyond mere supposition."

"I cannot disagree," said Cosden. "But why did the Dark Man give you these powers? Did he fear you?"

"Unlikely," said Okami.

"Then why?" asked The Professor.

"There was a deal in place," said Okami.

"And that was…" pressed Cosden.

"When my gifts were amplified I knew this man spoke true to his word. So when he told me something else that seemed impossible, I knew he meant it."

"And what was that?" asked Kokoro.

"He told me that I could possess a palace. An impenetrable fortress complete with a luscious forest that would be perfect for hunting. But I could not stay in 18th century Japan to possess this fortress. He told me that I would be taken several hundred years into the future. He said my palace would be on American soil but it would otherwise be exactly as I could dream it."

"What did you tell him?" asked Cosden.

"I told him yes, of course. Do you not see me sitting here before you?"

"What about the people who previously lived on this land?" asked The Professor.

"Oh yes," Okami recalled. "He informed me that two elderly individuals once occupied the land. Both were of immense power he told me. One was known as The Professor. The other known as The Clinician."

"So you know that this is my land?" The Professor asked.

"Naturally," Okami smiled. "Strike that—WAS your land."

"How long ago was that?" Cosden asked him.

"He transported me to the period I am in today. He informed me that he would be overhauling the entire population. He would be altering the entire geography. The construction of my fortress took eight years. The lush forest that occupies my backyard took just as long."

"Eight years!" said Kokoro.

"We were only gone for a few hours," said The Professor. "But the Dark Men used that distraction to savage our world."

"But how?" asked Cosden. "How can eight years elapse across the span of four hours?"

"Because time is relative," said Kokoro. "And wholly subjective."

"As I told you before," The Professor looked to Cosden, "time can be distorted and bent in every way imaginable and every way unimaginable. With the right knowledge and tools, it can be swiftly sped up or frozen and slowed down to make one hour last one billionth of a second."

"Because it doesn't really exist," said Okami. "It's purely a construct, a fabrication of the begetter. Like everything else. So what cannot be distorted?"

"Perhaps if everything can be distorted then nothing can

be distorted," Cosden said.

"Yes," said Okami. "But only if distortion occurs to all objects at the same rate. In which case, distortion becomes a form of normativity. But that is not what has occurred here."

"I've just realized something," said Cosden.

"And what is that?" asked Okami.

"Something I've not realized until this very moment."

"Explain!" Okami demanded.

"You possess enhanced abilities granted to you by the Dark Men. But I suppose that's the plural form. So your powers were granted by the Dark Man in the singular form. Regardless, you are not his creation."

"I have never labored under the delusion of being his creation," scoffed Okami.

"Be that as it may, if you are not his creation… then you are mine."

"I am of the creator, the begetter. But the begetter, you are not."

"That," Cosden told him, "is where we differ."

"So that is the delusion *you* continue to labor under," Okami sniveled.

"But I can't control you," Cosden said. "Not like I can others. But the reason I can't control you has nothing to do with a lack of abilities of my behalf. It is because you possess a portion of the Dark Men within you."

"The potency of my skills are now mine and mine alone."

"But that's not all I realized," said Cosden.

"Feel free to share these nuggets of wisdom," Okami laughed.

"Sure, my prose is not as polished as yours and The Professor's and Kokoro's. But I have also realized that, like them, you are also a manifestation of mine."

"Ridiculous!" Okami spat.

"The Dark Men keep you from seeing it. But it is clear to me that you are the manifestation of raw power and endowment—*My* manifestation of raw power and endowment. Do you know what that means, Okami?"

"Inform me, oh creator," Okami said with deep sarcasm.

"It means that you must become one with me. And if you aren't willing to join me as The Professor and Kokoro have, then I'll have to use force."

Okami laughed and laughed. Then he held his belly and laughed harder.

"I'm afraid the delusion runs deeper than I expected," Okami continued to laugh. "You really believe you possess a force that can match my own? Surely you jest."

"I have a question for you," The Professor said sternly.

"Go ahead." Okami finished laughing.

"What did you do with the other person who occupied this land?"

"The Clinician?" said Okami. "Your wife, correct? For the past 8 years I have kept her in suspension. The Dark Man informed me that he had no use for her."

"How dare you!" The Professor shouted. "Where is she!?"

"It's rather amusing," said Okami. "I never thought it would actually happen."

"What would?" asked Cosden.

"The Dark Man informed me that a young man along with an elderly fellow and a Japanese girl would one day show up to my fortress. He informed me that I should let them in. Dine with them, explain whatever they needed explaining. He told me they would be in search of power. And then he told me, when they show up, to kill them. That was the deal. That was the bargain."

"So the Dark Men set up an elaborate trap that took them eight years to get to this," said Cosden. "And they're not even the ones to do it."

"I'm afraid the Dark Men underestimated even me," said Okami. "Because I will do far more than kill you. There is great power in this room—that which is both ethereal and temporal. I will drain each of you; consume each of your powers. Then I will be more than illusory. I will be more than a projection. If there is only one mind in existence that can control the heavens and the earth, I will make sure that it is mine."

"That's not possible," said Cosden. "You are who you are. You can't change your perspective from projection to fully integrated mind."

"Ah," said Okami. "But you can."

"He's lying," said The Professor. "That or he's mad. Probably a bit of both."

"Fools!" Okami spat. "I will find a way to cultivate my consciousness into the begetter's. And it begins by depleting each of you."

Okami laughed as the table began to shake. The plates trembled and the bowls clanked against one another. Then suddenly all of them vanished from the room instantaneously.

Cosden looked down at his feet. He was standing in a pile of leaves. He was in a gigantic lively green forest of cracking trees.

"Professor!" he yelled out. "Kokoro!"

"There's no one to save you now!" a booming voice called out. Cosden recognized it as Okami's. Then he spoke again—

"WELCOME TO MY JUNGLE!"

Cosden looked around and Okami was nowhere to be found. Only his imposing voice was heard. And it echoed throughout the jungle as if it were a hollow cave. But this was no cave. The sun was shining bright. The wind was blowing. And Cosden was in danger. But he hadn't fully realized to what extent until a sword swooped in his direction.

A samurai sword was traveling at immense speed as it chopped through the leaves and trees of the jungle. It went darting directly at Cosden's head. He ducked at just the right moment and the sword spliced into a tree behind him.

"Who's there!?" Cosden asked.

The booming voice of Okami bellowed with laughter.

"Professor!" Cosden called out again. "Anyone!"

No one answered. Minutes went by with Cosden peering around his new environment. The sunlight beamed in his eyes and heated his skin. It was hot enough for him to quickly remove the jacket he was wearing and use it to wipe the sweat from his face. But he remained in the same area of the jungle until he heard heavy breathing behind him. He wasn't quite sure what it was. But he knew it was large. He could tell from its breathing that it was a creature of immense ferocity. He almost didn't want to know what it was. He didn't want to turn around and find out what was behind him. But he knew he had to. It was life or death.

Cosden reluctantly turned around. His worst fears had come true. When he turned around he realized where the heavy breathing arrived—a grizzly bear. It was standing upward on its hind legs and matched the height of two men combined.

"Easy boy," Cosden said as he slowly held his arms out.

The bear huffed.

"I don't want trouble."

The bear tilted his head down.

"Good boy," Cosden whispered as he slowly stepped away from the bear.

Then the bear's head tilted upward. Its eyes matched with Cosden's.

"Don't," Cosden said intently while still backing away.

The grizzly bear opened its mouth and roared with the ferocity of all the world's anger. Then it dropped to all fours.

"Oh no," Cosden said to himself.

The bear dug its clawed paws into the forest dirt and shot towards Cosden. As soon as it began running after him, Cosden took off. He was moving faster than he had ever run before in his life. He quickly glanced around to see just how close the bear was to him. The bear was gathering speed and moving faster and faster. But Cosden was able to outrun it. Cosden was darting through the scorching hot jungle with a bear at his heels. His confidence and knowledge was allowing him to move faster than a grizzly bear. Because on some level, he knew that he controlled the bear. Like everything else, it was a part of his world. The sun, the trees, the leaves, and the bears—they were all Cosden's to control. Even if he had not fully realized how to control it all.

Cosden pushed past trees and leapt over logs while the grizzy bear tore through everything in its path. It wasn't just moving quickly like Cosden. It was on a warpath. The grizzly bear didn't bother maneuvering around trees, it simply knocked over and shredded through every tree or branch or log it came in contact with.

After outrunning a bear while moving faster than any other human, Cosden stopped when he reached a long winding river. He was moving so quickly that he didn't spot the large body of water until it was too late.

What do I do! What do I do?

Immediately, the ferocious bear rammed into Cosden. The bear's head smashed into his back. He felt as if he had been hit by a freight train at full speed. The impact was so significant that he went flying through the air and splashed directly into the river.

Cosden was dizzy for a moment. The blow had sent him into disarray. He stood up, soaking wet, and climbed to the other side of the river. When he finally reached dry land, he fell to the ground coughing. He had to catch his breath and remove the water from his lungs. But the moment he looked up, he spotted the grizzly bear in the distance. Cosden was still lying on the ground when the bear charged at him for the second time.

The bear picked up immense speed and charged directly at Cosden. In a flash, Cosden jumped to his feet. He wasn't going to outrun the bear. Not this time. He closed his eyes and allowed every force within him take over. He allowed every ethereal force within him The Professor had told him about to take over.

The grizzly bear roared and Cosden stopped the wild animal in its tracks. When Cosden opened his eyes, he realized the feat he was achieving. He had the bear in his grips and was holding its mouth open. One of his hands held the bear's upper jaw while his other hand held the bear's lower jaw. The bear pushed forward and swiped at Cosden. One of its paws tore into Cosden's side.

It's now or never, he thought to himself.

With great strength Cosden ripped the bear's jaws apart, severing its skull and killing it instantly. The bear fell to the ground.

"Don't worry," Cosden told the lifeless bear. "You become one with me."

He extended his arm to the bear and the bear's body began to disintegrate. The lifeless bear transformed into thousands of particle-like substances, which were absorbed into Cosden's palm.

The wound from his side healed instantly as the essence of the bear pierced his being and became one with his collective subsistence.

What now? Cosden thought to himself. *How do I get out of here?*

"You are not done yet," Okami's voice whispered throughout the forest.

Cosden looked around and saw no one.

"Where are you!?"

He received no reply.

"Show yourself, Okami!" he called out again.

"Soon," said a slow whisper that flitted through the air.

Cosden pressed forward through the forest. A half hour later he was still slowly walking along what he felt was an endless journey. The sun radiated as his skin grew hotter with each step.

He walked for another hour. He wasn't sure how he was going to rescue The Professor or Kokoro. He wasn't even sure if Okami would ever show his face. Perhaps Okami would leave him in this suspended forest for all of eternity.

Why couldn't he make it out? he wondered. After all, this was his universe. This was his mind. But something within the forest was keeping him shackled. He could outrun the bear, but he could not outrun the trees. If Okami ever showed himself, Cosden would make him pay.

Who am I kidding? Okami is the strongest warrior in the universe. But if he's a manifestation of me, why can't I control him?

He thought further. *If I could outrun the bear and kill it, then I'm not completely powerless. Just need to get out of here.*

But how?

Another hour passed and the rays from the sun felt brighter and hotter than ever. Then Cosden began to feel…

Light-headed.

Must keep going.

So hot.

Need water.

Can't give up.

Slow steps.

Large forest.

Or jungle?

So hot.
Hungry.
Tree ahead.
Berries.
Approaches tree.
Plucks berries.
Notices other fruit.
Leans against tree.
Eats.
So good.
Apples.
Bananas.
Blueberries.
Strawberries.
Countless fruits.
All on one tree?
Large tree.
Tallest in the forest.
Must be…
The tree of life?
Arbor vitae.
Bites into strawberry.
Juice. Cold. Sweet.
Intoxicating.
Takes further bites.
Where has this tree been all my life?
Still lying against tree.
Still tired.
But fruit…
So good.
"Keep eating," said a whisper.
Yes.
Best fruit I've ever tasted.
So good.

Need rest.
The sun's rays refuse to rest.
So hot.
More than fruit…
Need water.
Cosden listens.
The sound of pouring…
Water!
But where?
Nearby.
Other side of tree.
Walks to other side of tree.
Flowing from tree.
Water!
Places mouth near tree limb.
Water pours into mouth.
Delicious!
So cold.
So fresh.
Places head under water.
Guess I could stay here…
With fruit and water.
But still…
So tired.
Must be…
Hot sun.
Can hardly…
Stand.
Falls to knees.
Bites into plum.
What a beautiful tree.
Going to take nap.
NO.
Can't stop.

That's what he wants.
Must go forward.
But where?
Doesn't matter.
Just forward.
Will take an apple with me.
Plucks apple from tree.
Continues moving through forest.
Slowly.
Minutes later.
Sun… so hot.
No more water.
Just as tired.
Stop for a nap.
Maybe.
No.
Can't.
Must move…
Forward!
Slow steps.
Wipes sweat from face.
Bites into apple.
Juicy.
Delicious.
Ripe red.
And…
Tired.
Eyes flutter.
Finally shut.
Drops to ground.
Eyes open.
Can't stand…
Too tired.
So hot.

Need water…
Need…
Rain.

Suddenly, it began to rain. Droplets fell against his face and slid across his forehead as he fell into a deep sleep. The last thing he saw was a raindrop splash into his palm as he dropped the apple. The last thing he heard was the sound of feet bristling through the forest.

**

"Wake up!" a voice called out.

Cosden yawned and wiped his eyes. Then he felt a stick poke him.

"Ouch!" he said as he slowly pulled himself up in a sitting position. "Who did that?"

Cosden looked around. Wherever he was, it was dark. He was inside somewhere. And directly outside it was not just raining but completely pouring down. Then Cosden realized what type of structure he was in: a cave.

Then he looked around and spotted an old man with the longest and filthiest beard he'd ever seen. He looked as if his beard were an unwashed bird's nest. The man's hair was just as bad and he wore rags that resembled potato sacks.

"Were you the one who just shoved that stick in my side?" Cosden asked him.

"Yes," the bearded man answered.

"Well, it hurt!"

"Sorry. Had to get you awake."

"But I had already yawned and awoken when you stuck me."

"Semantics!"

"Alright," Cosden said angrily, "forget the stick. Who are

you? Where am I? And why does it smell so awful in here?"

The odor was putrid.

"You're in the same place you've been for the past three days," the old man told him. "You're in Okami's forest."

"What do you mean three days?" Cosden asked. "I just took a nap for a few minutes."

"Few minutes! Ha! You were asleep for the past seventy-four hours, twenty-seven minutes and fifty-one seconds by my estimate. Not that I have a watch."

"You're insane."

"I'm precise," said the old man.

"If you don't have a watch then how do you know that? Good guess?"

"No," the old man informed him. "I am The Time Keeper."

"What does that mean?" Cosden asked.

"Later!" said The Time Keeper. "It is imperative that first we discuss you."

"What?"

"I found you immediately after you fell asleep in the grass. I knew you were here. It's the only reason I left my cave."

"What? You don't leave the cave."

"Later!" the old man told him. "This is first about you."

"Alright then, Time Keeper. Why did you help me?"

"Because you are the begetter. But you are facing dark forces. That which even you do not control."

"Okami?"

"No," said the Time Keeper as he scratched his ratty beard. "The Dark Men. Far worse than Okami. For you, at least. That's not to say Okami isn't unpleasant. I'm hiding from him, but I digress."

"No, tell me more!" Cosden answered.

"Can't... right now. Must continue with you for four hundred and thirty two more seconds. The fruit. It's what made you sleep for so long."

"But isn't that the tree of life?" Cosden asked.

"No, it's a forgery. A copycat. A cheap imitation. When The Dark Men gave Okami this forest, they bequeathed him the tree of life. Okami destroyed it entirely. Well, except for this…"

The Time Keeper reached into his pocket and pulled out a clump of soil laced with a few seeds. He placed it in Cosden's hands.

"For the begetter," said The Time Keeper. "Place it in your pocket. Keep it safe."

"Why would Okami want do destroy something so precious? Why would The Dark Men give it to him and not keep it for themselves?"

"Because only a soul of truth and a heart of light can pick from the tree of life. So for them, it would serve no purpose. I managed to salvage a few seeds, at best. But with the right care, the breadth of its branches shall thrive again… one day."

"Thank you," said Cosden.

"No. Thank you, oh begetter. Although this rain has been quite depressing these past few days."

"What do you mean?" Cosden asked.

"You wanted rain, did you not? That is what you asked for before you fell asleep. Well, it has been pouring down for the past three days. Seventy-four hours, thirty-two minutes and twenty-two seconds to be precise."

"How do I make it stop?" Cosden asked.

"I don't know. They're not my abilities." The Time Keeper shrugged. "I can only account for time."

"So can we finally talk about you?" Cosden asked.

"Yes, sure! It's about that time."

"Where did you come from?"

"From you, of course! Like everything that isn't of The

Dark Men, I am of you."

"What does that *mean*?"

"I have been around just as long as you have. Time is a fundamental and necessary structure, as least by my accounting. I've always been here. But I didn't yet become a physical entity until you structured the Paleolithic period. Later I was known by the name Gottfried Leibniz."

"I don't need to know what name you went by," Cosden snapped. "Basically I want to know how you can help me get out of here."

"Oh dear," The Time Keeper replied.

"What do you mean 'oh dear'?"

"I mean, if you're looking for a way out, you've got the wrong man, I'm afraid."

"You said you wouldn't have left this cave if I weren't out there."

"Yes."

"Why?"

"Two years, four months, sixteen days, twelve hours, forty-six minutes, and twenty-eight seconds is how long I've been here."

"That's fine and all. But that doesn't explain why," Cosden laughed.

"Because I am The Time Keeper, for goodness sake!" he shouted quietly before clasping his hands to his mouth.

"You've explained to me how long you've been in this cave. I'd like to know why you haven't left for so long."

"Why!? Didn't you have to outrun a bear a few days ago? Do you think I could do that? Heavens no. It's a jungle out there. It's far more pleasant to reconnoiter in here."

"I'm just wondering," Cosden said before he stopped speaking in order to observe the old man.

The Time Keeper stood from his sitting position as the rain continued to pour heavily outside. He paced around the cave, picking up sticks that were lying on the cave's ground. After a minute he had about two dozen sticks stuffed in his hands. Then he placed them in the middle of the cave and picked up a rock.

"What are you doing?" Cosden asked.

The Time Keeper didn't reply. Cosden watched as the asinine old man rubbed the rock harshly against his own hand.

"Careful, you'll hurt yourself!"

Cosden looked up through the cave's entrance and noticed there was little light out among the harsh rainfall.

"Voilà!" The Time Keeper jumped with glee. His hand produced a small fire from the rock rubbing. He quickly placed his hand into the pile of sticks, removed it, and shook the fire from his fingers as it transferred to the bundle of sticks.

"Mission accomplished, I guess," Cosden said. "Didn't know that was possible with a hand."

"Something I learned during the Paleolithic period. Thank you."

The fire embers both lit up the cave and provided warmth from the harsh weather.

"But back to what I was asking before you started that fire. What's so special about this cave? Why is this a good hiding spot from Okami? This is his forest, right?"

"Yes, this is Okami's forest. But this is my cave."

"What does that mean?"

"I built this cave. It was never a part of Okami's forest. It is exclusively mine."

"What's that got to do with him finding us in it?"

"Okami could never find us in here because, as I've told you, this is my cave and I'm The Time Keeper."

"I'm still not understanding."

"Okami is unable to find my cave because I've hidden it

through time. This cave may exist in this forest, but it exists on another plane of time that is beyond the temporal dispatchments limited to Okami. Thus he is, in effect, never able to find me nor it."

"Incredible. So you have the power of hiding things in plain sight by shifting them across the plane of time—the fourth dimension, right? So you can hide things in a fourth dimension only you have access to."

"Or you."

"Me?" Cosden asked.

"I am a personification of yours, after all, dear begetter."

"Right. So I can do this as well?"

"This is a power you bestowed upon me. You are certainly capable of it, but I would need to become one with you."

"And how does that happen, Time Keeper?"

"Quite easily. The same way the ferocity of the bear became one with you after you killed it seventy-four hours, fifty-nine minutes and thirty-six seconds ago."

"So I just sort of absorb your being?"

"Exactly. But it's slightly more complicated right now. Such an act can't occur across this plane with such an imbalance."

"What do you mean such an imbalance?"

"Why, I've been hiding in this cave in this forest for the past two years, four months, sixteen days, thirteen hours, eighteen minutes, and twenty-four seconds. Haven't you noticed that time has been rather off lately? It's because I've not been in action. I've been hiding from Okami. It's why so much time was able to lapse from the time you and The Professor first went to Nazi Germany and the time you returned. Without me controlling order, The Dark Men were able to impose their own monstrous impositions upon the temporal."

"So your plan was just to stay in this cave for eternity?"

Cosden asked.

"Eternity? No, no, no! Just until this blew over. Perhaps another fifty to one hundred years or so."

"You're kind of insane," Cosden laughed.

"I don't know," The Time Keeper replied with a straight face. "I don't get out much."

"That bit is obvious."

"But I'm certainly glad the begetter is here to chat with me. I suppose the next hundred years won't be so lonely after all."

"Look here, you kook." Cosden stood up as the embers hosted his shadow against the cave wall. "If you think I'm going to stay cowering in this cave for years on end, you're dead wrong. The moment I have a plan of attack and the moment this rain slacks up, I'm out of here."

"Brave! So brave." The Time Keeper began rocking back and forth near the fire.

"And haven't I mentioned how horrible this cave smells? You never explained why."

"Sorry, I think that smell is probably our dinner."

"Dinner!?" Cosden asked.

"Yes, the bear you killed. I've been eating it for the past few days. I'll cook a little more now, if you don't mind."

The Time Keeper jumped up and darted toward the back of the cave. He emerged with a large sack. When he opened the sack it was the worst smell Cosden could ever imagine.

"My god," Cosden said. "No refrigerator in here?"

The Time Keeper laughed. "Good joke, that one."

"Surely there's got to be a better way to preserve it."

"Nope," The Time Keeper replied.

He pulled out several chunks of raw meat from the sack.

"Already skinned it," he smiled while scratching his beard with his free hand.

"Terrific," Cosden said sarcastically.

Then The Time Keeper pulled a skillet from the bag and placed the meat onto it.

"You just had that skillet lying in the same bag as that smelly old meat?" Cosden asked.

The Time Keeper shook his head. "Uh-huh."

Then he sat back down in his previous spot and held the skillet over the fire.

"Is this how you do it each night?"

"Correct."

"What did you eat before this bear?"

"Sometimes I'll allow a squirrel or a muskrat to wonder in here just so I can turn it into lunch."

"Oh."

"Well, I've been keen on the muskrat lately. But a bear is great because it'll last for days! I'm afraid I wouldn't fare very well while attempting to kill a bear. So I'm thankful you're here. If you stay long enough, perhaps I'll get to cook a little muskrat for you. Do you prefer it rare or medium?"

"Have I already mentioned that I think you're insane, Mister Time Keeper?"

"You may have mentioned it once or twice."

"Thought so."

"But I am made in your image after all. So I cannot take offense with such a comment. If I am insane, then so are you. What am I but a small part of you? One of the many parts that equal the totality of your sum as begetter."

"Lovely," Cosden said sarcastically. "I continue to hear this but don't feel like much of a creator. I don't even recall doing any creating."

"Oh, you don't need to recall it for it to have happened. Perhaps it was an unconscious effort. No one remembers what he or she thinks or does unconsciously. I don't think."

"Do you need some help there?" Cosden asked.

"With what?"

"That skillet."

"Sure."

"Let go of it," Cosden said.

"Are you going to grab it? I don't want to it fall in the fire and burn our dinner."

"Trust me. Let go of it."

The Time Keeper slowly removed his hands from the handle and Cosden made the skillet hover over the fire without being held.

"Incredible," The Time Keeper said. "Who could doubt you?"

"I was just thinking," Cosden said.

"Yes." The Time Keeper listened intently.

"How could I have created a thirteen and a half billion year old universe when I only just turned 24."

"And you figured I would have an appropriate response because I am The Time Keeper?"

"Yes, basically."

"Then allow me to ascertain. There is nothing rigid about time. It is constantly in flux—and from my plane, it is never ending. There is no past, present, or future. There is simply a series of vertices from which anything can be retrieved. Every second of time is constantly occurring. Your perspective is only limited to the plane in which you are looking from. Perhaps you hopped from one plane—one dating back 13 billion years to another—one dating back 24 years. Age is a relative factor that hardly applies to you, of all people. You are, in essence, no more 24 years old than you are 13 billion years old."

"I certainly hadn't thought about it like that."

"And the creation of the universe is hardly a valid measure of your age. Your mind could have existed an additional 10 billion years before the creation of this universe."

"I suppose that's enlightening."

"Well, don't give it too much thought. The possibilities are limitless—but these are just guesses on my behalf. My expertise lies only with time. And that is why I can only make assumptions regarding your position."

"Why?" Cosden asked.

"Because you are of the time before time. When you envisioned time, you envisioned me. I cannot tell you what came before. I believe myself to be your first creation of this universe. So if I cannot provide an answer, then no one can. Besides yourself."

"So you're saying I should ask myself questions?"

"I believe you already have. And I'm certain you will in what you refer to as the future. I can see it now. You will be standing directly in front of yourself—discussing these very complexities."

"Right," Cosden said half-heartedly. "Sure."

"I know it sounds one step removed from absurd but at this point, you know you should not doubt that which appears absurd. It is likely more true to your senses then that which appears practical and pragmatic."

"I have a question," Cosden asked.

"Yes?" he answered, scratching bugs out of his beard.

"Why not just speed up time until Okami has perished?"

"Why not speed up time!?" he repeated Cosden's words.

"Yes."

"Surely, begetter, you recall the title bestowed upon me."

"The Time Keeper," Cosden said.

"Yes. The Time Keeper. Not The Time Maker. Or Time Manipulator. Just The Time Keeper."

"So you can't."

"No, I cannot control time. That is neither my purpose nor function. I am here to look over time. To understand it. To keep it from derailing. Not to control it. I am its guardian, not its manipulator."

"So you're powerless?"

"Of course I am powerless! A man of power does not spend two years, four months, sixteen days, thirteen hours, forty-three minutes, and thirty-four seconds hiding in a cave!"

"I guess that makes sense."

The Time Keeper burst into a fit of laughter.

"Forgive me," he said, still chuckling. "Humor must be found somewhere. Not many laughs to be had in a cave so I cherish the few."

"I could use a good laugh too," Cosden agreed. "I mean, I'm in a cave preparing to eat a bear with you, after all."

The Time Keeper moved closer to the fire. He grabbed a stick from the ground and poked around the meat in the skillet.

"Almost ready," he said.

Then he grabbed a few leaves from his pocket, ripped them up, and sprinkled them into the pot.

"What's that for?" Cosden asked.

"Flavoring. The leaves are deciduous. Nice and frothy."

"Sounds awful," Cosden laughed.

"See, I told you a good laugh helps."

The Time Keeper then grabbed two old clay cups from a second bag that was lying on the ground.

"We'll drink from these," he told Cosden.

Then The Time Keeper walked toward the entrance of the cave. He placed the two cups out in the pouring rain and waited for them to fill up.

"Rain water," The Time Keeper said as he pulled the cups back in. "Delicious. The salt gives it just a pinch of flavor."

"Thanks," Cosden said as he grabbed a cup of rainwater and took a small gulp.

"You like it?" The Time Keeper asked.

"No," Cosden answered earnestly. "Not at all. It's awful,

in fact."

"You'll get used to it."

"No," he asserted. "I won't. I'll be out of this cave in no time. I'm not going to spend two years and ten million months in here like you."

"Touché."

The Time Keeper plunged a sharp stick into a piece of cooked meat, removed it from the skillet, and placed it on a thin wooden plank. Then he handed it to Cosden.

"Bon appètit."

The Time Keeper quickly scraped together his own helping and scoffed it down. Cosden, in contrast, was hesitant. But he was also hungry. So he took a bite into the darkened bear meat.

"What do you think?" The Time Keeper asked.

"It's okay, I suppose."

"Honestly?"

"Yes," Cosden answered. "It's enough to get by on if you're cowering in a cave for the remainder of your life."

"Yes," The Time Keeper laughed as chunks of meat fell into his beard. "That's precisely how I look at it."

"I have another question for you," Cosden told him.

"Yes?" The Time Keeper responded.

"What do you know about The Dark Men?"

"Likely less than you." The Time Keeper gave a weak smile.

"Tell me."

"The Dark Men are far worse than Okami," said The Time Keeper.

"Have you met them?" Cosden asked.

"Yes."

"What were the circumstances?"

"Not the most pleasant. That I can say for sure. You see, the Dark Men understand that time is relative to one's plane

—one's point of view. They understand that if you can alter your plane of existence, then you can alter the perception of time. That is where I came in. They hunted me down many years ago. They found me in the alpine mountains. I had been hiding there for four years, six months, two weeks, three days, nine hours, and forty-nine seconds when I left the mountain to find food. That is when they apprehended me. They tortured me, searching for the secrets to manipulate time."

"Secrets you never knew in the first place. Because you don't manipulate time."

"Precisely. They will need you in order to fully manipulate time from the singularity."

"The singularity?" Cosden asked.

"The point at which time began. Everything can be controlled from that point. And only the begetter can reach that point."

"That's why they want me?" Cosden asked.

"Among other reasons. Your abilities are discernably unlimited, after all. I suppose that would make anyone a desired commodity."

"They seem undefeatable."

"To those of us who do not possess certain attributes, sure. But to you? Eliminating the Dark Men should be a priority."

"I promise, it is. I just don't know how to get rid of them. They've ruined everything. But I want to know why they placed you here."

"Well, I was of little use to them. So they threw me to Okami. He placed me in his forest as he does many others. He uses this forest as a sport for his hunting ground. He generally gives his prey two days in the forest before he hunts them non-stop. On the second day I created this cave and placed it within the remnants of the space-time dimension which Okami is unable to see. So he's never found me. He was irritated at first but eventually gave up after tossing countless others in here."

"Countless others?"

"Well, that's an exaggeration to be sure. My estimate is forty-nine since me."

"Forty-nine people he's hunted in here since you've been in hiding?"

"Yes."

"And you said that he hunts after two days?" Cosden clarified

"That's correct. He always starts after two days. Hours, minutes, and seconds may vary but an average count of seven hours, thirty-two minutes, and twenty-three seconds."

"So that means he's out there hunting for me right now?"

"Of that I am certain," The Time Keeper said. "That's why it's so much more pleasant in here."

"I need to know… how do I defeat him?"

"Strength, courage, ferocity, and perhaps animalistic fear. The same traits that he possesses. That is what it will take to defeat him."

"Where will I find him?" Cosden asked.

"This far into his game, you'll never have to worry about finding him. He'll happily find you. In fact, he's likely irritated at his inability to find you right now."

"I think it's time for this rain to slack up," Cosden said. He shoved his plank of charred meat down on the cave floor and the rain outside immediately went from pouring down to nonexistent. Then the skies were lit with light.

"Did you just do that?" The Time Keeper asked.

"I did."

"Astonishing. What now?"

"I find Okami. I defeat him. Then I get The Professor, Kokoro, and The Clinician back."

"Wait," The Time Keeper stopped him. "What about The Dark Men?"

"What about them?"

"How will you defeat them?"

"I don't yet know."

"Think," The Time Keeper said. "Think."

"It's impossible to defeat just one at a time. They multiply."

"Yes. So what do you do then?" The Time Keeper asked.

"I don't—Ah. I got it."

"Yes?"

"I need to get them all together. Each and every one of them."

"Yes!" The Time Keeper said with glee.

"And when they're all together in one place, then I destroy them."

"Brilliant!" The Time Keeper clapped. "That is precisely what you need to do."

"I just need to figure out how," Cosden replied.

"You will. You will know precisely what to do when the time is right."

"Thank you," Cosden said. "Now it's time I got out of this cave. I'll see you when Okami's body lies at my feet."

"That is a meeting I will very much look forward to."

Cosden stood tall and exited the cave. He made his way out into Okami's forest in the bright of day. This time he was ready for battle.

Minutes later, Cosden found himself in the middle of the forest. Trees, daylight, and the chirping of birds surrounded him.

"Show yourself, Okami."

"As you wish," a voice said softly.

Cosden turned around and standing in front of him at a distance was Okami.

"I've been searching for you, Mister Ke."

"And I, you."

"Where have you been, Mister Ke? A cowering spot most hidden, to be sure. Hardly the actions of the begetter."

"I thought you doubted my role as creator?"

"I still do. My tone was meant to be that of mock and ridicule, Mister Ke."

"Why do you doubt me?" Cosden asked.

"Because I have met the begetter. You may look like him. But you are not him."

"I may look like him? You're insane, Okami. The Professor, The Clinician, Kokoro, and The Time Keeper all know exactly who I am. But you do not."

"The Time Keeper?" Okami said with intrigue. "He is still around?"

"He's been hiding in this forest for over two years," Cosden answered.

"How is that possible? This is my forest and I know every area of it. I never found him."

"There are many realities you are apparently unaware of, Okami. But this ends here. And it ends now."

"How can you be so sure, Mister Ke?"

"Because I have no intentions of dueling with you beyond the perimeters of this forest. I'm afraid this is the end of the line."

"Your arrogance is blinding. Your followers have blown both your abilities and ego totally out of proportion."

"This is coming from the man who calls himself the world's most unstoppable warrior."

"I am worthy of my title, Mister Ke. The same cannot be said of you. It is true that this ends here and now. But only for you."

Okami drew a samurai sword from his holster. He held is squarely in front of his face and pointed a finger toward Cosden's feet. Cosden looked down and spotted a sword.

He picked it up.

"My battles are a display of my feat," Okami told him. "It would be a disservice to offer you anything but the finest sword. You will need it, after all. Not that it will offer much help."

"We'll see."

Okami and Cosden both simultaneously took a slight bow. Then Okami rushed toward Cosden like a high wind blowing through a wheat field. Okami's sword was immediately met with Cosden's own. They clashed like ancient warriors on a battlefield.

Their swords were clashing back and forth at a fiery rate—

Left.

Right.

Center.

Above.

Lower left.

Upper right.

Overhead.

Right.

Down.

Lower right.

Left.

They backed up from one another—each breathing as heavily as the other.

"We've only just begun," Okami said with a grin.

"I'm counting on it," Cosden responded with just as much vigor.

Okami rushed toward him at the speed of wind as their swords clashed back and forth once more in a duel to the death—

Up.

Down.

Left.

Right.
Right.
Corner left.
Front.
Lower right.
Left.
(DUCK)
Above.
Far right.
Behind.
(Steps back)
Right.
Left.
Center.
Front.
(FASTER)
LeftRightCenterFrontLowerRightUpperLeftOverhead.

Finally they backed away from one another to catch their breath.

"You are skilled, Mister Ke. But are you no Okami."

"We'll see."

Okami rushed at him once more. But this time, when Okami swung his sword at him, Cosden ducked and Okami's sword plunged into a tree. Okami quickly attempted to pull his sword out to no avail. Cosden held his own sword at Okami's neck.

"You've lost. And far quicker than I'm sure you thought you would."

Okami used his foot to swiftly kick Cosden's sword out of his hand. Then he ran toward Cosden and hit him with a blow that knocked him to the ground. Okami then slammed his fist to the ground as Cosden quickly rolled out of the way. Man-to-man, face-to-face, and fist-to-fist they exchanged blows back and forth.

Cosden was moving faster than he ever thought he could. And he was fighter far better than he ever thought he could. Every other second he held up his forearm to block a blow from Okami. They went back and forth with fists and feet.

Left.

Right.

Uppercut.

Elbow.

Left.

Left.

Forearm.

Right kick.

Left kick.

Left punch.

Right kick.

Forearm.

Elbow.

Left chop.

Right kick.

Okami threw a left hook at Cosden. He ducked and knocked Okami to the ground with an uppercut. Cosden quickly picked his sword up and held it at Okami's throat once more.

"The second time, Okami. You've lost."

"The loser of this fight, Mister Ke," Okami hissed, "will be decided by the corpse that cannot move."

Cosden heard a noise grow from faint to loud in the span of two seconds. He turned around just as a rhinoceros gored him to the ground. Cosden tumbled to the ground and was reeling from the same feeling of being hit by a car speeding at 100 miles per hour.

Cosden stood to his feet and quickly grabbed his sword. He looked around and noticed Okami was out of sight. The rhinoceros, with its intimidating tusk, slammed its feet into the ground.

"Okami's sent you to finish me off."

"This is my jungle," shouted Okami's voice.

"You couldn't fight me yourself!" Cosden shouted. "So you send in more animals!"

Okami's voice spoke no more.

"You know it's the truth, Okami!" Cosden continued to shout. "You can't do it yourself! But it makes no difference!"

Cosden gripped his sword with all his might.

"Nothing personal, rhino," Cosden turned to the animal. "But you're in the way of The Professor."

The rhinoceros stampeded toward Cosden as he rolled out of the way and sliced one of the rhino's legs. The animal screamed in pain.

"One leg down."

The rhinoceros ran toward him again. He sliced another of its legs as the rhino plowed into a tree, knocking it over and erupting the entire forest. The rhino grunted and again ran toward Cosden. He attempted to slice its back leg but this time the rhino managed to strike him in the side. He fell to the ground.

"You are no match," Okami's voice called out from afar.

"Why not finish this yourself!" Cosden yelled out.

"I shall," Okami's voice whispered.

Then the two thousand pound rhinoceros leaped onto Cosden, who quickly lifted his sword into the air. The blade pierced the rhino's heart. The animal grunted loudly and died instantly. Then all of its weight fell onto Cosden.

"Ah!" Cosden yelled.

He was being crushed by two thousand pounds of dead weight. With all of his might, he pushed the animal off of him. Then he stood up as the heard the roar of Okami. Almost intuitively, Cosden grabbed his sword from the rhino's heart and swung it behind him. When he turned around, he discovered his sword had been plunged into Okami's chest.

Cosden twisted his blade, pulled it out, and Okami fell to the ground. Dead.

Then Cosden closed his eyes. He took a deep breath as Okami's body dissipated into a million particles and became one with him.

"Is it all clear?" called a voice.

Cosden turned around and spotted The Time Keeper.

"All clear," Cosden whispered.

"The sun. The fresh air. The trees," The Time Keeper said. "It's all so beautiful."

"Thank you," Cosden said.

"You did it? You killed him?" The Time Keeper said.

"No," Cosden said. "I would never kill my own creation. Even if it's been distorted by the Dark Men."

"I suppose that's a nice way of putting it."

"It is the only way of putting it," Cosden told The Time Keeper.

"He tried to kill me!"

"He tried to kill me, as well. But Okami in his previous form is no longer burdened. He's one with me now. As it should have been."

"And so should I," said the Time Keeper. "I'm much too tired in this form."

"Very well," said Cosden. "But before you do, there's just one more thing."

"Yes?"

"I now hold Okami's strengths and attributes. As well as his memories. He mentioned that he had met the begetter—who looked like me but wasn't me. Now that I hold his memories, there he is—meeting me from years ago. But I do not recall such a gathering."

"I imagine you've met many people," said The Time

Keeper.

"That is true. Perhaps we met while I was a university student and unaware of my current position."

"As ruler of the universe?" The Time Keeper said.

To that, they both laughed.

"Are you ready?" Cosden asked.

"Ready and set."

The Time Keeper closed his eyes. He wilted into a million pieces and absorbed into Cosden's palm.

"I remember," Cosden said to himself. "Everything."

With the feats of Okami and the knowledge of The Time Keeper, he walked down a steep path through the forest. He walked as if he knew exactly where he was going—because he did.

Finally he arrived at the backdoor of Okami's fortress.

"Open," Cosden said with one hand held out. The doors flung open. But he didn't immediately enter. He stopped right outside of the door and turned to face the forest. He reached into his pocket and pulled out the clump of soil and seeds The Time Keeper had given him. With his hand, he scooped up a bit of dirt from the ground and placed within it the soil and seeds that would grow into a new tree of life.

"Rest well," he told the seeds.

Then he turned to the fortress and entered through the doors. Cosden walked down a hallway filled with Japanese artifacts and opened a door on the left. Inside was The Professor, The Clinician, and Kokoro.

"You're here!" Kokoro said.

"I knew you'd do it," The Professor told him.

"Most wonderful," clapped The Clinician.

"I am pleased to see each of you, as well," Cosden told them. "Most pleased."

"What happened?" Kokoro asked. "Where is Okami?"

"You defeated him," The Professor said.

"He's a part of me now. All of him but the traces of The Dark Men."

"Terrific," said The Professor. "You're stronger than ever before."

"I am," he agreed. "I can feel it. It's almost serene."

"There remains much work to do," The Clinician told him. "Do not become content when adversity remains a threshold to overcome. The Dark Men are out there... among others."

"I couldn't agree more," Cosden said.

"We must remain steadfast," The Professor added.

"So what is next?" Kokoro said.

"How about we discuss it over supper?" The Clinician said.

"Sounds good," Cosden nodded. "The last thing I ate was bear meat prepared in a cave."

"What?" Kokoro half-laughed.

"I'll explain over dinner."

And so he did. Hours later, they were all in the dining hall for a feast. When Cosden entered, he was dressed quite differently. He was wearing white robes.

"That's quite a look," The Professor told him.

"It's what I'm meant to wear," Cosden smiled. "I quite like it."

"Robes fit only for a begetter," Kokoro added.

"I'm afraid it's going to take quite a bit of alteration to get this place back to our humble abode," The Clinician said, changing the subject. "This old castle has got to go. Yes, yes, yes. It cannot remain."

"I was beginning to like it," Kokoro laughed.

"It's certainly roomy," said The Professor.

"It's much too drab," The Clinician said as she took her first bite of food.

"The meal is delicious," Cosden told her. The others

agreed.

"Oh, don't thank me," she laughed. "The kitchen here contains an entire team of cooks."

"Then we offer our thanks to them," Cosden said as he raised his glass.

"What else did you learn during your time in that forest?" The Professor asked Cosden.

"Most importantly, I realized how the Dark Men might be defeated."

"Well, tell us!" Kokoro rushed him.

"They must be destroyed together. As one. Luring one away, blasting him with lightning, will do no good. We need all of them in the same spot. I just need to know where I might find them. It's the only worthwhile battle."

"They scatter constantly," Kokoro told him. "Finding all of them in the same spot—improbable."

"Nor do I know how such a method could be accomplished," said The Professor.

"Do you have any ideas?" Cosden asked The Clinician.

"I'm afraid not," she said. "My knowledge does not extend to such boundaries. But I am aware that the decision you make in the near future tells me that an answer is imminent."

"But how can it be imminent if there is no one here who has an answer?" Cosden said. "Even after all I've learned, this is one that eludes me."

"Perhaps there is someone else we can turn to," Kokoro said.

"Professor," Cosden said. "Are there are other personifications out there who might be able to help?"

"Are there other personifications? Yes. But would any of them know how to harness The Dark Men in a single spot, I am uncertain."

"There must be someone who knows," said Cosden.

"There is!" called a voice.

They all turned around. Standing at the door of the dining room was Hosuto, the right hand man of Okami.

"I know," Hosuto said.

"How can we trust you?" Kokoro asked.

"I am bound to serve Okami. Whose soul has been grafted to Cosden Ke. So it is Ke who my allegiance remains faithful to."

"I don't want a servant," Cosden told him. "I only want to know where to find all of The Dark Men in one spot. Help me do that, Hosuto. Then you are free from servitude."

"If that is your desire then I shall fulfill it, Mister Ke."

"You will lead us to the Dark Men?" The Professor asked.

"You know how to do that?" Cosden questioned him.

"No. Not exactly. I know not of the Dark Men's whereabouts. But I know the person who does."

"Who would that be?" Cosden asked.

"The Map Maker," Hosuto answered.

"Who is that?" Cosden asked.

"The Map Maker is the individual who guides the geography of this planet and of this universe. The Map Maker understands everyone's locations at any given time. The Map Maker is the architect of direction."

"Great," Cosden said. "And you'll take us to him?"

"Her," Hosuto corrected him.

"You'll take us to *her*?"

"Yes. I shall."

"When should we leave?" Kokoro asked.

"How about the morning?" Cosden asked.

They all nodded.

"Then it's set," said The Professor, "We'll travel to meet The Map Maker in the morning."

Hours later, Cosden stood outside the fortress. It was dark out as he stared into the stars, wrapped in white robes. He stood motionless until Kokoro joined him.

"Beautiful, isn't it?" she said.

He nodded.

"And it's all yours. Constructed and maintained by you."

"I remember the beginning. I remember it quite vividly."

"Which beginning?" she asked.

"The beginning of... everything."

"So you remember it all?"

Finally he moved his gaze from the stars and looked to Kokoro.

"Not all... I... I can't remember The Dark Men."

"Even with The Time Keeper instilled in you, you can't remember their beginnings or how they got here?"

"No. I can't remember where they were derived from nor when they arrived. But I think the reason I can't remember is because I never knew in the first place. The Dark Men are parasitic. They don't belong here. They were never a part of this vision. They're here by force and they've begun to cloud everything."

"So it is imperative that we find The Map Maker."

"Yes, I think so," Cosden nodded.

"And you think if you can get The Dark Men—all of them, in one spot—you can permanently stop them?"

"No, I don't know," Cosden said. "I don't even necessarily think so. But I hope so."

"Is that what The Time Keeper told you?"

"No. It's what I told myself."

"Cosden, you said they cloud everything."

"Yes."

"To what degree?"

"I'm not sure if it's possible to delineate a spectrum of obfuscation to the matter," Cosden replied. "I just don't know."

"You're beginning to sound like The Professor," she told him.

"Am I? Forgive me. I suppose his language is rubbing off on me."

"That's one way to look at it," she told him.

"What's another?"

"To assume you're undergoing the inevitable eventuality."

"Of what?" he asked.

"That which you do not need to be told," she smiled.

"I knew you'd say that."

"I want you to come with me," Kokoro told him.

"Now?"

"It'll only take a moment."

"Sure," he said.

"You're not going to ask me where?"

"No, Kokoro. I'm not. Would you like to know why?"

"Why?"

"Because I trust you."

Instantly they zapped from the exterior of the fortress to the interior of the fractal palace. It was just as cold blue in hue as it was the last time they visited. And there along the familiar walkway of the fractal dome were countless doors aligned along a never-ending row.

"It's calm in here," he told her.

"Serenity," she whispered.

"I've been wondering…"

"Yes?" she said.

"I now have the sight of The Time Keeper. So why do I need this palace of fractals?"

"You have already answered your question. You have attained the *sight* of The Time Keeper. This palace, with its infinite number of doorways, is purposed to alter and correct that which you see from The Time Keeper's plane of view."

"So The Time Keeper allows me to see. This palace allows me to act."

"Precisely."

"Why didn't I think of that?" he asked.

"You did. What am I but another of your personifications?"

"So," Cosden laughed. "I've been talking to myself this entire time."

"That's one way to look at it."

"I find myself now often thinking—does it matter? My prior lack of knowledge did not alter the knowledge itself. It merely altered my…"

"Perception?" Kokoro said.

"Yes," he smiled somberly. "That's the word I'm looking for."

"Glad to be helpful."

"So, Kokoro—why did you ask me here? Surely our chat could have continued right outside the fortress walls."

"You said you trusted me."

"I do," he added.

"Then follow me."

Kokoro opened a door on the left that looked exactly like all the others. She walked through it and Cosden followed after.

As they entered the other side, Cosden noticed that he and Kokoro had stepped inside a diner. And not just any diner, but the kind that belonged in a small rural town made of citizens who'd lived in the same small houses on the same neighboring streets for the duration of their lives. It was a diner as old timey as humanly possible.

A large waitress burst from the kitchen with a tray of plates in her arms. She placed two plates in front of an elderly couple sitting at a table, each bespectacled with Coke-bottle glasses and clothing made of wool so fine it appeared to be handmade to the untrained eye.

"Here y'all go," the waitress. "Bacon platter for the young man. Eggs and sausage for the young lady."

"Wonderful! Wonderful!" said the husband.

"Oh, it looks delicious," said his wife.

"Y'all enjoy now," the waitress wagged a gleeful finger. "And do tell if you need anything else."

"Yes," said the husband. "A little ketchup would do well."

"And some jam," said the wife.

"What flavor?" asked the waitress.

"Strawberry's my favorite," said the wife as she sliced a knife into her eggs.

"Comin' right up," the waitress said as she whisked away.

Cosden turned to Kokoro. He was getting ready to ask her the purpose of taking him to a diner when the front door of the diner opened. In walked a middle-aged man wearing a suit and fedora. He carried in his hand a briefcase, while a small numbered card was stuck in the brim of his fedora hat. Everyone turned and stared. The man waved and smiled before taking a seat at a table near the elderly couple.

"Why look'a'there, sweetie," said the husband. "It's that news reporter from Channel 2."

"Are you sure that's him, darling?"

"I sure am. That's him alright."

"Well will ya look at that," the wife gasped. "It sure is."

"Wonder what he's doing in a small place like this," the husband whispered.

Instead of whispering back, the wife waved her hand in the air in order to grab the reporter's attention.

"You're that fancy news reporter, aren't ya?" she asked.

"I sure am," he answered. "Reporting from Channel 2."

"Oh, how lovely," she said. "Nice to see you mingling with the little people."

"Well, this is my home." He smiled a grin so wide that it could have been replaced with a large sterling banana.

The waitress approached the news reporter.

"Why hello there, Mister News Reporter. What can I do

for you?"

"Coffee, toast, sausage," he smiled. "In that order."

"Coming right up."

Finally Cosden turned to Kokoro.

"What is this?" he asked her.

"This is not reality," Kokoro answered.

"What do you mean?" he asked.

"This is a vision."

"People eating at a diner. How mundane could a vision be?"

"What word did you just use?" she asked.

"Mundane," Cosden answered.

"Is that not precisely what The Dark Men desire?" Kokoro asked rhetorically. "Do you think anyone at this diner ever questions reality? Ever questions normalcy or homogeneity?"

"No explanation, no evaluation, no justification needed," Cosden said. "These are individuals who have never attempted to go beyond the wire framework that traps them. Nor have they ever desired to do so. They are the ultimate subjects."

"To question reality is the first step toward taking action. All people are made in your image. While they can be subjugated, they can also be liberated."

"And The Dark Men don't want that," Cosden said.

"They do not," Kokoro answered. "They seek the rigidity of order. What you are witnessing is a vision of what The Dark Men initially desire. There is no liberation if you fail to eliminate them."

"You said this is what they *initially* desire," Cosden said to her.

"Yes."

"What do you mean by *initially*?"

"Follow me," Kokoro gestured as she walked through a door that stood in the middle of the diner. Cosden followed right after her and they found themselves back in the fractal palace.

"I asked what you meant by 'initially'," Cosden said.

"And you will see quite soon," she answered. "There is one other door we must visit tonight."

"Where might that be?" Cosden asked.

"Take a look for yourself."

Kokoro opened another door and Cosden entered after her. This time they found themselves on a pavement road during the day. The road was filled with old abandoned cars, which were riddled with bullets or torn into pieces.

"What is this?" Cosden asked.

"Look," Kokoro told him.

She pointed to a figure in the distance. Two men were running towards them. One was an accountant type. The other was a store clerk identified by his wardrobe. The men stopped near a bullet-riddled car.

"None of the cars are working," said the clerk.

"No gas, no cars, no food around here," said the accountant.

"There's a store roughly four down," said the clerk.

"Four miles down? I can't go that far. My wife is somewhere out there. So's my daughter."

"If you left them behind, it's too late," the clerk told him.

"I never left them behind," the accountant said angrily. "I was working. Suddenly the police showed up. Faceless, nameless, they attacked everyone. They made everyone an offer—shackles or death."

"How did you get away?"

"I snuck through the exit hatch of our office building. I rushed home to find my family... No one answered."

"You think they were taken?" the clerk asked.

"I have no idea," said the accountant. "I pray they're safe. Waiting for me. Somewhere."

The two men began searching the cars for food.

"That was two days ago," the accountant continued.

"I was at the bakery," the clerk told him. "Faceless officers showed up. Guns blazing like the Gestapo. I ducked and managed to get away. Bodies were everywhere."

"Why would they do this?" the accountant asked.

"Don't you realize?" the clerk asked. "It started long before this. First were the curfews. Then they stripped us of voting powers. Then they stripped us of free speech in the name of maintaining order. Now this."

"We sat back," the accountant said to himself. "We let this happen. You're right. Things have gone from bad to worse. Now officers can kill without purpose—anyone they want."

Sirens began blaring down the street.

"We've gotta get out of here!" the clerk yelled.

The two men turned down a corner street. Cosden and Kokoro, who could not be seen, followed after them.

"In here!" called out a voice.

The accountant and the clerk spotted a woman at the front door of an abandoned store. Each window was boarded up with wood.

"In here!" she said again.

The accountant and the clerk spotted the woman and ran inside the defunct store. Kokoro and Cosden, still unseen, followed right after them. The interior of the store was filled with men, women, and children. All of them were extremely quiet.

"Thank you," said the clerk.

"We heard sirens. They almost had us," the accountant told her.

"You're welcome," said the woman. "I'm the manager here. Or at least I used to be. Before the officers blew through town."

"How many people are in here?" the clerk asked.

"As many as I can gather," the manager told him.

"Honey! Are you in here, honey!?" the accountant yelled out.

Immediately a woman and young girl ran to his arms and the three of them embraced.

"You're alive!" the wife said. "We were looking everywhere for you!"

"Shhh!" the manager whispered to them. "You've got to keep it down. They're out there looking for us."

The accountant turned back to his wife. "I went to the house after the police raided the office. I couldn't find you anywhere. I wasn't sure if you two were safe or not."

"I love you, daddy," the young girl said as she hugged him.

"Love you too, pumpkin."

"Are we just going to stay in here?" the clerk asked.

"For now," the manager told him. She walked over to a cabinet and pulled out a shotgun. "We've got to stay safe. We've got the pantries stocked so there's enough food. With you two, there's now about thirty-six people in here."

"What about the others? Out there..." the clerk stumbled for his words.

"I'm afraid they're on their own. If I see 'em come near the store, I'll invite them in. Otherwise, I can't save everyone."

"But there's so many out there," said the clerk.

"Then you feel free to step out there and rescue them," the manager sneered.

The clerk scoffed.

"I didn't think so," the manager laughed angrily.

"Who do you think is behind all this?" the clerk asked her.

"Not who. *What*," she said. "They have no faces. No soul, no heart, no values but what they make. I don't know what they are, but there's got to be a way to stop them."

"This is no way to live," the clerk said. "We can't just spend our entire lives in an old building with boarded up windows."

"This is a quick fix!" the manager shouted quietly.

"You've got a gun. You can take them on."

"You must be kidding, kid! You think a single gun is going to take out countless police officers with razors for hands? We're going to need a better plan than that."

"I'm sorry," the clerk said. "I was a little too hasty. You're right. We'll need a strategy."

"Right. We'll need to know how to take 'em down."

"I saw someone shoot one of the faceless officers several days ago. The thing fell to the ground with its police helmet on and didn't move. So we know they can be killed."

"God help us if they couldn't," the manager said.

Their conversation was interrupted when the ground *shook*. Everything in the store rattled and several shelves turned over. Then the doors of the store burst open.

Faceless police officers stood in the doorway. The thirty-six people in the room began screaming.

"No," Cosden said to Kokoro. "I have to stop this."

"No," Kokoro said. "Don't."

She placed her hand against Cosden's chest to keep him from interfering.

Blades withdrew from the arms of The Dark Men as the survivors in the store screamed for their lives. A faceless officer dashed up to the clerk and stabbed him in the chest. Life lifted from his eyes as his last breath was drawn. The officer retracted the blade from the clerk as the manager used her shotgun to ward the Dark Men away.

"Out of my shop!" the manager yelled.

Screams.

Shots.

Stabs.

Lives were lost.

The officers slashed people left and right until they made it to the manager. She died instantly. Cosden attempted once more to move forward.

"No more," he said.

Suddenly, everything stopped. The screams, The Dark Men, the constant movement. It all stopped.

"I would not allow you to interfere," Kokoro told him. "Because this is not reality."

"What are you talking about? I'm seeing it with my very eyes." Cosden told her.

"What you're seeing is a possibility of a future with the Dark Men."

"This is a simulation?" Cosden asked.

Immediately, everything around them disappeared and the environment transformed in a wireframe model.

"Simulation is not the word I would use," Kokoro told him. "It's a signifier of artifice."

"But what I just witnessed could come true?" Cosden asked.

"Yes," she answered. "At first the Dark Men remain contempt with order over that which you created. But things change as they find lesser value to human life—to all of existence. They will eventually seek to wipe out and exterminate anything that isn't them."

"The power of control can only take them so far," Cosden contemplated.

"Precisely," Kokoro agreed.

"Thank you, Kokoro. I now realize the importance of this mission. More than I did prior to *this*."

"I knew you would need it," she said as they walked back through the fractal palace and then into the exterior of the fortress. "Now rest, if I might offer a suggestion. We've a map maker to find in the morning."

***

The next morning, Cosden, The Professor, Kokoro, The Clinician, and Hosuto were gathered outside of the fortress. It was bright, sunny, and warm.

"What a lovely day out," The Clinician said. "I think I'll tend to the garden today."

"You won't be joining us?" Cosden asked.

"Heavens no," The Clinician laughed. "I've too much work to do in terms of restoring my estate from his awful fortress."

"Then I guess we'll see you once we return," said Cosden.

"I promise I'll have transformed this place back to normal by then," she smiled.

The Clinician hugged Cosden and gracefully swayed through the garden and out of sight.

"See you later, my dear!" The Professor waved to her.

"Is everyone prepared?" Kokoro asked.

"We're only going to search for a map maker. How difficult could it be?" Cosden asked.

"I must warn you, Mister Ke, it will not be an easy feat. The Map Maker is guarded," Hosuto warned him.

"Guarded by whom?" Cosden asked him.

"By her protectors."

"Dark Men?" Cosden asked.

"No," Hosuto answered. "She is guarded by men neither light nor dark. The forces guard her."

"The forces?" Cosden asked.

"The forces that craft the language of the universe."

"I guess I'll see for myself when we get there," said Cosden.

"If everyone is prepared then we shall proceed immediately," Hosuto told them.

They each nodded.

"Very well. Let's go!" Hosuto shouted. In a flash, they were all warped through space and time. They disappeared from the grounds of the fortress and found themselves pushing forward through rays of light, which cascaded in every direction. Two seconds later the four of them were transported to a vast desert wherefrom the sun's rays were much warmer. The desert sand was golden brown, flaky, and left deep footprints.

"Where are we?" Kokoro asked.

"This place feels familiar," The Professor said.

"Welcome," said Hosuto, "to the Danakil Desert located within the Afar Triangle covering northeastern Ethiopia."

"Ethiopia?" said Cosden. "We're a long ways from home."

"Undoubtedly," said Hosuto. "After you, gentlemen."

"What does that mean?" Cosden asked.

"We have a short walk to take," said Hosuto. "This is as close as one can teleport to The Map Maker's whereabouts."

"Then we'd better get a move on it," said The Professor as he strutted forward. The others soon followed.

The rays of the sun were kind to no one. Thirsty, dry, and hot—they walked for nearly a mile, leaving four pairs of heavy footsteps behind them, when Cosden stopped.

"Is anyone thirsty?" Cosden asked.

They all shouted "YES" in unison.

"Why hadn't I thought of this sooner," Cosden said rhetorically.

Cosden closed his eyes, allowed his mind to rest, and the ground began to shake. The desert sand parted near Cosden's feet and a fountain erupted from the ground.

"Incredible," Kokoro said.

Then desert sand began to pour from the fountain. Gold, flaky, dry sand.

"That's no use to us," said Hosuto.

"Wait for it," Cosden told him.

The sand pouring from the fountain miraculously transformed into cool spring water. The water overflowed from the fountain as the four of them drank from it.

"A thing of beauty," The Professor said before gulping from the fountain.

Kokoro splashed water on her face and enjoyed every sip, every taste, and every feel of the coolest water in existence. But when she looked up, she spotted something that caught her attention and made her forget the fountain she was drinking from. It was a large black sphere that sat in the distance.

"What's that?" Kokoro said quietly.

No one answered.

"Over there!" she shouted much louder.

They turned to look at the sphere in the distance.

"An orb of some sort," said The Professor.

"That is it," said Hosuto. "We're nearly there. That is the location of The Map Maker."

The miraculous fountain in the desert was soon abandoned as they headed toward the direction of the giant sphere. It sat in the sand and was the height of a five-story building. There were no windows and no way to see inside the sphere. It was a shining flair of ebony and could have been a stand in for a black hole. After several more minutes of walking, they stood directly in front of it and were awed at its breadth.

"She's inside there?" Cosden asked.

"Yes," Hosuto answered. "Somewhere."

"Somewhere?" The Professor asked.

"We'll have to do a bit of searching to find her," Hosuto informed them.

"It's a giant black orb," Kokoro remarked. "Would she not be at its center?"

"There is only one way to find out," Hosuto scoffed. "Just... be prepared."

"How do we get inside?" Cosden asked.

"That is not my expertise," Hosuto answered.

"What does that mean?" Cosden asked. "How is that helpful to me?"

"Few wield the ability to open this sphere," Hosuto said. "But you are one of those few. If Okami could do it, then surely the man who defeated him can."

"Very well," Cosden nodded. Then he placed his hands out and closed his eyes. He took a deep breath and freed his mind. Then a part of the sphere that touched the ground sprang open like a door.

"You did it!" Kokoro told him.

Cosden opened his eyes and spotted the small entrance into the orb.

"Let's go before it closes," The Professor said.

The four of them rushed into the sphere. Hosuto was the last to enter and the entrance shut shortly after. Inside, they found themselves in a small room with only three walls that ran like a triangle. Each wall was covered in thin lines, both horizontal and vertical—like graphing paper.

"What is this?" Cosden asked.

"Of that, I am unsure," Hosuto answered. "The interior was completely different when I arrived here with Okami many years ago."

"The interior was different?" Cosden asked.

"It is my understanding that the inside of this sphere changes each time one enters. Therefore the individual is less likely to find The Map Maker."

"She doesn't really want to be found very often, does she?" Kokoro said lightheartedly.

"Men have died in here and gone mad in their search for The Map Maker," Hosuto answered.

"The Map Maker is presumably busy," said The Professor. "And doesn't often like to be disturbed. So she's hidden within the walls of this funhouse."

"A funhouse this is not," Hosuto said.

"There are only three walls in this room," said Cosden. "What an anomaly."

"Curiouser and curiouser," Kokoro whispered as she looked around.

"So what do we do in here?" Cosden asked.

"Of that, I am unsure," Hosuto answered.

"It's a puzzle," said Kokoro. "There's something here that must be answered."

"Well, let's take a look," Cosden said as he clasped his hands together.

"We've three walls," said The Professor. "But I'm not sure they're all equal."

"What do you mean?" Cosden asked.

"I mean I think each of these walls is of a slightly different inclination."

"How do you know?" Cosden asked again.

"Somewhat intuitive. Somewhat visual. A keen eye can see something's not quite right about the angles of these walls."

"Fascinating to say the least," Hosuto said.

"Why are the walls lined?" Kokoro asked.

"Good question," Cosden told her. "Perhaps it's a key."

"I suppose we could count up each square, line, and tile made by each wall to calculate the difference. But it would take a while," The Professor told them.

"Surely you know a more convenient method than that, Professor," Hosuto scoffed.

"Alas, I am a Professor of philosophy and not of mathematics. Sorry to disappoint."

"Let's see if I can figure this out," Cosden said. "We have three walls total as opposed to the more traditional four. That means we're inside of a triangle inside of a square. We believe that each wall is of a different inclination than the next so…"

"So if that applies to all three walls then we are located within a scalene triangle," said The Professor.

"Terrific," said Hosuto. "But knowing what type of triangle we are being held in is of little help to escaping."

"Maybe it is," said Cosden.

"We just need to know how one breaks free of a scalene triangle," said The Professor as he rubbed his chin.

"Maybe," said Kokoro, "we just need to find the perimeter."

"The perimeter of a triangle is the sum of each side," said Cosden. "A plus B plus C."

"So we'd need to measure each side as I originally tasked," said The Professor proudly.

"That should do the trick," said Kokoro.

Hosuto began counting, "1…2…3…4…5…6…7…8…"

"What are you doing?" asked Cosden.

"Counting each tile."

"That could take all day," Cosden said. "And what if you're off by a few numbers? Start completely over?"

"With all due respect, Mister Ke," Hosuto said, "if you've a better idea, please volunteer it."

"Guess I'd better count the second wall and someone start on the third wall," Kokoro said.

"I don't wish to spend the remainder of my life within the confines of a small triangle with the likes of you all," Hosuto said.

"And we, you," The Professor laughed. "No wonder you said men have gone mad in here. Who dare blame them?"

"Who constructed this, Professor?" Cosden asked. "The Dark Men?"

"Heaven forbid," The Professor said. "Doubtful."

"The Map Maker constructed this," Hosuto answered.

"To keep men away."

"And The Map Maker is a personification of mine?" Cosden asked for confirmation.

"Affirmative," said The Professor.

"Then that means…" Cosden paused.

"It means that you are the creator of this sphere," The Professor's face lit up.

"And if it is a creation of mine, then I should be able to manipulate it to some degree," Cosden continued.

"Precisely," The Professor confirmed.

"Then let's give it a try, shall we?"

Cosden stretched an arm out and the vertical and horizontal lines on each wall began to merge. The countless lines swarmed together and formed a single vertex on each wall—a small dot that glowed brightly as the rest of the walls stood void and blank.

"1… 2… 3," Kokoro counted.

"3 vertices," Cosden informed them. "Forged by withdrawing the intersections of each wall."

"Your abilities are astonishing, Mister Ke," said Hosuto.

"I must concur with Mister Hosuto," said The Professor.

"A vertex on each wall," said Kokoro. "But what to do with them?"

"To calculate them, of course," Cosden said.

Each vertex began spinning against the wall. They began spinning so fast in clockwise rotation that each vertex stretched into a wide flattened oval that resembled a miniature black hole.

"What are they doing?" Kokoro asked.

"Spinning," said Hosuto.

"Beyond that!" Kokoro snapped.

"They're computing," Cosden told them. "Computing all that they've absorbed."

Then the vertex orbs-turned-ovals began to slow. They

decelerated for several seconds before coming to a complete halt. And from each of the three black ovals rose a number.

The longest wall held the number "77"

The second longest wall held the number "64"

The shortest wall held the number "39"

"There it is," The Professor said. "The inclination of each wall. 77 degrees. 64 degrees. And 39 degrees. Three very different inclinations as I predicted."

"What are these?" Hosuto said.

"Answers," Cosden said. "These are the numbers we should need to get out of here—but nothing is happening."

"We must be missing something," said. Kokoro.

"I think I know what we need," The Professor told them. "One person stand against the smallest wall. One person against the next smallest. And two people against the largest wall. That should balance everything out."

"Come on," Cosden said to Kokoro as the two of them stood against the longest wall.

The Professor stood against the wall labeled "64" and Hosuto stood against the wall labeled "39."

"Now what?" Hosuto asked.

Nothing happened for a moment and just as Hosuto was prepared to speak again, the room began to shake.

"What's going on!?" Hosuto began to panic.

"Steady everyone!" Cosden said as the room continued to shake.

The wall that Cosden and Kokoro were standing against began to shorten horizontally. Kokoro took a step away from the wall but Cosden grabbed her hand and pulled her back against the shaking surface.

"Steady," he said again. "No one's going to get hurt."

"How do you know that?" Hosuto said as his wall began to horizontally increase.

The Professor remained calm and stable as his wall, like

Cosden's and Kokoro's, began to horizontally shorten. Then the shaking came to an abrupt standstill. They all looked around and to each of them it was apparent that the three walls were now different in size. The calculated numbers that arose from the flattened ovals disappeared.

"That's it!?" Hosuto said. "We remain in the same room following that?"

"There's certainly been some change," Kokoro said. "Each wall has altered in length and structure."

"Everything looks a bit more even about now," The Professor said.

"Let's do a little calculation, shall we?" Cosden said.

He stretched out an arm and the flattened ovals began to spin again. They grew larger as they moved faster and then grew smaller as they moved slower. Then they came to a halt once more and revealed three matching numbers: "60."

"60…60…60," said The Professor. "The perfect triangle."

"A total of…" Cosden said.

"180," Kokoro answered.

"What next?" Hosuto answered.

"I don't know," Cosden admitted.

"Each wall is now equal in degrees," The Professor looked to Cosden and Kokoro. "But there are two of you against that wall."

Cosden stepped away from the wall. He moved to the center of the room as Kokoro, The Professor, and Hosuto stood against each of the three walls.

"Open says me," Cosden whispered.

Against The Professor's wall, light emitted in the trace of a tall door that flew open.

"Lead the way," The Professor said heartily to Cosden with the flick of his wrist.

Cosden entered through the door followed by Kokoro, The Professor, and Hosuto.

"Finally!" Kokoro said as she entered the door before realizing where they'd end up.

The four of them were now in another white room—this one looked different. This room contained four walls but each wall was lined with the same vertical and horizontal thin lines that resembled graphing paper. And, like the triangular room, each wall looked disproportionate in length.

"This again," Cosden said. "Ridiculous."

"Ha," Hosuto laughed. "Surely you did not think The Map Maker had only one room to decipher. With our luck, there may be one hundred."

"Unbelievable," said The Professor. "One hundred?"

"We'll surely die within the confines of these walls," said Kokoro.

"I speak in hyperbole, but the point is understood," Hosuto told them.

"So we're in a new room," said Cosden, "and this one has four walls. Much more traditional. But each of the walls look just as scattered and uneven as they were in the previous room. "

"Do your thing," Kokoro nodded.

"Yes, you'd better get a start on it before every oxygen particle is sucked up by Hosuto's big mouth," The Professor half-laughed.

"Perhaps you should stick with the philosophy, Professor, and stay away from the humor," Hosuto shot back.

"Both of you," Cosden pointed at them. "Now's not the time."

"Right you are," The Professor agreed. "We've much work to do."

In routine fashion, Cosden shut his eyes and held out his hands. The various lines began to converge and merge into a singular point on each wall. This, again, formed a small black sphere against each wall. Then the spheres began to rotate in a clockwise position and transformed into flattened ovals that produced numbers.

"48, 48, 41, 63," The Professor read the four numbers. "A total of 200."

"We have four walls," Cosden thought aloud. "Two sides are of the same inclination while two of them are of varying degrees of inclination. So we're not in a square."

"We're in an isosceles trapezoid," Hosuto clarified.

"That's right," Cosden agreed.

"So this room is unlocked by the same method as the last," said Kokoro.

"It appears so," Cosden answered. "We know the drill."

The four of them each stood directly against a wall.

"Open," Cosden said with assurance.

Nothing occurred.

"Open!" he yelled louder.

Again, nothing occurred.

"Why's it not working?" asked Hosuto.

"I don't know," Cosden said. "I must be doing something wrong."

"Four walls, four numbers," said Kokoro. "Perhaps there is a missing piece."

Hosuto stepped away from his wall opposite Cosden and something began to happen—his wall, and *only* his wall, began to shake.

"This can't be right," The Professor thought aloud.

Then the wall's movement ceased and from its black hole of an oval shot four spears. The four spears darted directly at Cosden's head. Kokoro let out an audible gasp until she noticed the spears were frozen in mid-air, inches from Cosden's face.

"Don't worry," Cosden told them, his hand in the air controlling the spears. "My reflexes are faster than ever."

"And for good cause," said The Professor.

All of them stood in awe at the four spears levitating in front of Cosden's face. He pushed his hand away and the spears slowly backed into the middle of the room.

"That could have killed you," Hosuto told him.

"As I said, my reflexes are beyond reproach. It is, admittedly, a relatively new phenomena."

"So that method no longer works," Kokoro said.

"Not for this room," Cosden seemed to agree.

"And the wrong move may set off a death trap," said The Professor.

"That too," Cosden said.

"We must act carefully and swiftly," The Professor nodded.

They slowly moved away from the walls and carefully looked around the room for further clues.

"Maybe something else can be done with the numbers," said Hosuto.

"Or maybe we need to stand in a different spot," Kokoro added.

"I don't see much," Cosden said as he peered across the entire room.

The metal spears remained levitating in the middle of the room and each of them were careful to avoid such sharp devises.

"There must be something more," The Professor said with his arms folded.

"I was just thinking…" Kokoro said.

"Yes?" The Professor answered.

"There is one of us for each wall. But what if only two individuals arrived here in search of The Map Maker? It would have been impossible to get past the first room without at least three people. And now four, apparently."

"An astute observation," The Professor nodded.

"Those are the men who would die in here," Hosuto answered her.

"Terrifying thought," Kokoro said.

"That is why a quest for The Map Maker will lead you down a path that mere mortals would not venture."

"No one else is this secretive or protected," Cosden said, frustrated.

"No one else is The Map Maker," Hosuto replied.

"Up there," Cosden said quietly.

"What?" Kokoro asked.

Cosden pointed to the ceiling. "Up there!"

They each looked up and spotted four glowing round marks on the top of the ceiling.

"What is that?" Hosuto asked.

"The real vertices," Cosden said.

"You found it," The Professor said. "Most brilliant."

"We have to touch each one of them to move forward," Cosden said.

"How do you know?" Hosuto asked.

"Intuition," Cosden nodded.

"The one thing you must never doubt." The Professor patted him on the shoulder.

"One problem," Kokoro said. "How do we get up to the ceiling of this room to reach each vertex?"

"The impossible question," The Professor said.

"Not at all," Cosden said. "Anything can be manipulated with ingenuity."

"You're the boss," The Professor smiled.

Cosden turned to face the four spears in the middle of the room. He pointed a hand out toward them and the spears began to shift. Each of them bended and contorted as if their molecular structure were being modified from the inside out. Suddenly the long metal spears had become large round plates.

"From spears to metal discs," Hosuto said. "Most impressive."

"One for each of us," Cosden replied.

The four metal plates lowered and levitated to their feet.

"Step on," Cosden told them. "Time to ride."

"An excellent idea," Kokoro smiled.

"Nothing's impossible," Cosden said. "Not when you're in control."

They each stepped on a metal plate and were immediately levitated upward. They were lifted far enough into the air to easily touch the four illuminated areas of the ceiling.

"This… is ingenuity," The Professor laughed.

The entire room, the walls, ceiling, and floor, all began to shake.

"Lower us!" Kokoro said.

Cosden quickly lowered each of the metal plates and the four of them hopped onto the floor. The room continued to shake—then it did more than shake. The room began to expand. Two parallel walls began to push outward. They pushed further and further until the room was stretched to twice its original size. Then the shaking stopped.

"After all of that!" said Hosuto, "And we are still stuck in the same room!"

"There must be more," The Professor said.

"Absurd!" Hosuto spat.

"Patience," Cosden told him.

"I'm beginning to think that the statement '100 rooms of puzzles and traps' was not hyperbolic," said Kokoro.

"Disheartening, undoubtedly," The Professor agreed. "But we must press on."

"What kind of room is this?" Cosden asked.

"Still four walls," Hosuto said.

"Two of which have extended outward quite a bit," Kokoro added.

"Let us count," said Cosden.

The black ovals pressed against the walls began to spin

and spin. Then the ovals moved into the four corners of the room and numbers appeared.

"90…90…90…90," said The Professor. "In each corner."

"That's four right angles," said Cosden. "But that only explains the corners. It doesn't account for the actual size in order to determine the perimeter."

Then the ovals began to move again. The four ovals formed into two ovals. One pressed against a long wall and formed the number "320" while another pressed against the shorter wall and formed the number "140."

"Wonderful," Cosden said.

"What can we do with this information," asked Hosuto.

"We can calculate it," said The Professor. "We are currently located within a rectangle. The two longest sides measure 320 while the two shortest sides measure 140."

"We calculate the perimeter of a rectangle by doubling each of those two numbers. That gives us 640 and 280. It's elementary," Cosden informed them. "Now add them together and we get…"

"920," Kokoro interjected.

"That's right," Cosden confirmed. "A total of 920."

"And we do what with this information?" Hosuto asked.

"I'm making this up as I go, Hosuto," Cosden answered him. "One step at a time."

"Very well. Just make it quick."

"I'd fare better, Hosuto, if you offered a larger variety of suggestions and a smaller variety of complaints."

"I will do what I can," Hosuto shot back.

"920," said Kokoro. "We need to apply this number in some fashion to this room."

"But how?" The Professor pondered.

"If we add up the numbers, we get eleven," said Kokoro. "But there's not eleven of us."

"Nor are there eleven walls," said Cosden.

"What if the number isn't meant to further represent geometry or mathematics?" The Professor said.

"What do you mean?" Cosden asked.

"What else could a number be used for, if not a mathematical equation?" The Professor asked.

"A year," Hosuto said.

"Of course!" Cosden agreed.

"The year 920?" Kokoro asked. "What significance could that hold?"

"Does anyone remember where we're located?" The Professor asked.

"Of course," Hosuto said. "I'm the one who brought us here. We are in the Danakil Desert located within the Afar Triangle of Northern Africa."

"Precisely," The Professor said. "Now think of the year 920 in northern Africa."

"That is a year with which I am not familiar," said Hosuto.

"Nor I," said Cosden.

"Fortunately, I am," said The Professor. "And so are you, Cosden. After all, what is my knowledge, but yours?"

"Just tell us already!" Hosuto said.

"920," The Professor began, "was the Middle Ages for Europe. But for Africa, the cradle of civilization, the year 920 was, in the northern region, known as the Golden Empire."

"Interesting," Cosden said. "But how does that help us?"

"My sentiments precisely," said Hosuto.

"The key words," said The Professor, "are 'Golden Empire.' What type of empire?"

"Golden?" said Cosden. "But again, I don't see how that is relevant."

"This room has granted us elements," said The Professor. "It would be wise to use them."

"What elements?" Cosden asked.

"Those spears you transformed into discs," said Kokoro.

"Thank you, Kokoro," The Professor smiled.

"But those spears or discs are silver," Hosuto scoffed. "Far from gold."

"Ah," The Professor said. "But who amongst us has the ability to alter the molecular structure of an item at its atomic level?"

"Cosden!" said Kokoro.

"That's insanity," said Hosuto. "Not that Mister Ke is unable to fulfill this task. But who else would be capable of such a feat? Does that make him the only one on earth currently capable of reaching The Map Maker?"

"I believe so," said The Professor. "That is the point after all. She has structured her sanctuary so that only the begetter can reach her. It would certainly prevent her work from falling into the wrong hands, such as The Dark Men."

"Enough small talk," Cosden said. "I've got to work to do."

Cosden outstretched his arm. The four metal plates came together like magnets and began to distort and shake and bend in every direction. The plates folded inward as their internal and external structures were destroyed and rebuilt. The others watched as Cosden's eyes remained closed—focused.

Cosden opened his eyes and the previous metal plates were now gold—shining and reflective. The four plates jumped into the air and one flew against each wall.

"920," Cosden said, "The year of the Golden Empire."

The others looked around with uncertainty.

"Open," Cosden spoke softly.

Against the wall furthest from them, a door emerged and swung open.

"You did it," said Hosuto. "Good job, Mister Ke."

"Let's go," Kokoro told them. "You don't know how long

it'll stay open."

The four of them quickly ran to the doorway and through it. Sudden they found themselves in—

Another. White. Room.

"No, no, no!" Hosuto shouted. "Not another one!"

"The previous room was only the second," said Kokoro.

"And this is the third!" Hosuto shot back. "What we seek may be found in the fourth room or it might be in the four hundredth!"

"We have no way of knowing," Cosden told them. "But there's something off about this room."

"Let's see," said The Professor. "How many walls are in here?"

Kokoro counted as she looked around the room. "1...2...3...4...5."

"Five walls," said Cosden. "First room had three walls. Second room had four walls. Now five."

"So we can expect the next room to hold six walls," said The Professor.

"*If* there is a next room," Hosuto reminded him.

"There will surely be another room," The Professor scoffed. "If we're lucky, it will host The Map Maker."

"And if we're not lucky?" Hosuto asked him.

"Then we'll likely find ourselves in another puzzle room with growing walls."

"I'm only concerned with this room," Cosden told them. "The first room was a shifting triangle. The second room was a trapezoid that transformed into a rectangle. Now we're within five walls which forms a..."

"A pentagon," Kokoro answered.

"But there's something else that's different about this room. More than just the number of walls or the size."

"Such as?" Hosuto asked.

"The lines," Cosden clarified. "These walls aren't covered

in lines like the first two."

"I'm glad you caught that," said The Professor.

"That means I can't manipulate the numbers to form a vertex," Cosden told them. "So I can only determine that the perimeter and measurements of this room are irrelevant."

"So these five walls must hold some other key?" Kokoro asked him.

"I believe so."

"Maybe, continuing from the previous room, there lies historical importance within these walls," The Professor thought aloud.

"Perhaps," Cosden said as he pressed his palms against the walls.

"I regret bringing you here," Hosuto answered.

"I have no doubt that you do," Cosden nodded once.

"Maybe you can reverse time," Hosuto laughed. "Turn back the clock and stop us from ever arriving here."

"I will do no such thing. But I am certainly curious as to ascertaining the ability to regress time itself."

"It is, of course, within your capabilities," The Professor told him. "So long as you harbor the fractal palace granted by Kokoro and the labors of The Time Keeper. With those two elements, you are in full control of time. But as with any object that powerful, I would suggest you exercise such actions with caution."

"Of course," Cosden agreed.

"So that means you won't thrust me out of here?" Hosuto asked.

"Not a chance," Cosden smiled. "Now help us find a way out."

"I think the oxygen levels have already begun to lower," said Hosuto.

"If that were true," said The Professor, "you'd have stopped talking."

"So we believe numbers to be of no use," Kokoro said as she changed the subject.

"Well, measurements, specifically," Cosden clarified.

"Perhaps there are others like gold or silver that could be useful," she said.

"No," said Cosden. "This room has not presented us with any items as the last room did. In fact, there seem to be no clues whatsoever in here."

"Abandon hope, ye who enter," Hosuto said desperately.

"No," Cosden said to him. "Why would you abandon hope when answers are so close?"

"Because we have no idea how many rooms lie ahead of us," said Hosuto. "We'll likely die of starvation before we make it to The Map Maker."

"How exactly did Okami make it to The Map Maker?" The Professor asked him.

"Okami is a warrior," Hosuto answered. "When I entered this place with him, there were no puzzles to answer, only battles to be had. That was many years ago. The Map Maker is now more secluded than ever. More fortified than ever."

"Hidden by intellect and not brute force," Cosden said as he looked around the room.

"And what a difference it makes," The Professor said.

"Kokoro," Cosden turned to her.

"Yes?"

"You said that maybe the walls were the key to moving forward."

"I did."

"What if the walls are not the keys," said Cosden, "but we are."

"The same way we unlocked the first room," said The Professor. "By standing against the walls in equal proportions."

"Exactly," said Cosden. "But instead of three or four, we

have five walls to bridge. Everyone get to a wall."

The four of them each stood against a wall. But there remained one empty wall.

"We're in a pentagon," said Hosuto. "So this cannot work. There are only four of us."

"We need one more person," said The Professor.

"The Map Maker has made this an impossible task," said Kokoro.

"Nothing's impossible," Cosden said to her. "The Professor told me that."

"If this is truly the key to progressing then we doomed," said Hosuto. "One cannot simply conjure up people from thin air."

"Or can one?" Cosden asked him.

"There exists numerous personifications within him," The Professor said.

Cosden closed his eyes and from him emerged a ghost-like figure. The emergence looked as if his soul were parting ways. The translucent figure that derived from him was The Time Keeper.

"Happy to help," The Time Keeper nodded to them. Then his diaphanous figure gracefully floated to the fifth wall of the room.

"Open," Cosden said. And another door swung open from fifth wall.

"There it is," said The Professor. "Let's go."

All of them, including the ghost-like Time Keeper walked through the doorway.

"Oh no," said Kokoro.

On the other side, they were astonished to find themselves in—Another. White. Room.

"We'll never get out of here!" Hosuto cried.

"Pull yourself together!" The Professor told him. "We've got to try."

"This is the last room before we make it to her," Cosden told them.

"How can you be sure?" Kokoro asked him.

"I feel it."

She looked around the room and counted the number of walls. "1...2...3...4...5...6."

"As expected," said The Professor.

"A hexagon," Cosen said to himself.

"This is asinine," said Hosuto. "I have no reason to trust your intuition. Your powers are proven but omniscient, you are not."

"That is true, Hosuto. I am not."

"I am turning around."

"You and I both know that is impossible, Hosuto," Cosden said to him.

Hosden turned his back to Cosden and began banging on the wall from which they arrived. Unfortunately, the door had both sealed shut and disappeared from sight.

"Let me out of here!" Hosuto demanded. "I want out!"

"There's no use for that," said Kokoro. "It's designed to keep you where you are."

"That is why I need to get out of here!" Hosuto.

"Hosuto, Please," said Cosden. "We need you. We need your help to get out of here."

"Then what do you suggest?" Hosuto asked.

"I assured you that this is the last room that is betwixt where we were and where we're going."

"So what do we need to do?" Hosuto asked him again.

"We need to reconnoiter against each wall as we previously did."

Cosden, Hosuto, The Professor, Kokoro, and the spirit of The Time Keeper each stood against a wall. This meant there were five walls down—one remaining.

"This is a hexagon," Kokoro said. "We need one more

person."

Cosden looked at her and smiled. Then he turned to Hosuto. "This one is for you, Hosuto."

He shut his eyes and a soft light beamed from within him. The light separated and revealed itself as the spirit of Okami. Floating and translucent, the spirit bowed.

"Master!" Hosuto yelled out.

The spirit of Okami turned to him and spoke. "You have made me proud, Hosuto."

Then he approached the sixth wall and stood against it. In an instant another door appeared and burst open. Okami and The Time Keeper both floated toward Cosden and became one with him.

"It is done," Cosden whispered.

Cosden, Kokoro, The Professor, and Hosuto all walked through the door. On the other side was not an empty white room—but a room filled with drawings, maps, compasses, and parchment scattered all over the floor and stacked in every area.

In one corner of the small room was a table scattered with more maps. Sitting at the table, drawing the maps, was a dark-skinned woman with long dreadlocks.

"Are you The Map Maker?" Cosden asked.

The woman looked up for the first time. She placed her pencil upon the small desk and looked to no one but Cosden.

"I am," she said. "And the sustainer has finally arrived."

"Me?" Cosden asked.

"Are you not the sustainer of all that which is celestial?" she asked, already knowing the answer.

"I've been called the creator and the begetter. First time I've heard 'sustainer.' But I modestly prefer to just be called by the name I was born with: Cosden Ke."

"The name you were born with?" she asked.

"Yes," he said. "It's all I've known for the past twenty odd years."

"Your current body is but one of many forms your soul has utilized over the billions of millennia."

"What do you mean?" Cosden asked her.

"You have taken many forms. A supernova here, a solar system there. A micron of bacteria, perhaps an Australopithecus, before you drifted to your current form."

"That's the first time I'm hearing of this," Cosden said to her.

The Map Maker stood from her desk and walked closer to Cosden.

"For just as long, I have been here mapping the whereabouts of everything. Waiting for this moment. To tell you just that—I suppose."

"You've been in this orb for millions of millennia?" Cosden asked.

"I am not The Time Keeper," she said modestly. "I haven't kept track of the dates as well as he. But the days certainly add up."

"That's a very long time," Cosden said.

"Time is a temporal construct," she answered. "Time is but the human's perception of a change in space. One man's millennium is another man's millisecond. I suppose it just depends upon which dimension you are looking through."

The Professor interrupted. "Pleased to make your acquaintance," he told her. "I am The Professor and from the moment you spoke it has been apparent to me that I am in the presence of a personification of immense knowledge."

"I would thank you," she said, "but my knowledge extends only to that which the sustainer has bestowed upon me. Nothing more, nothing less."

"You know these things only because it is your duty to know these things," said Kokoro.

"Precisely," The Map Maker answered.

"My name is Kokoro, by the way," she told The Map Maker. "Organizer of temporal events."

"So like me," The Map Maker said, "Your duties have been granted to you by the sustainer."

"Yes," Kokoro answered. "We are all personifications."

"Not I," Hosuto spoke up. "I am no personification. I am servant to Okami."

"Have we met?" The Map Maker asked him.

"Many years ago," Hosuto answered, "my master, Okami, entered this sphere and made his way to you. I was standing by his side. It was much different at that time."

"Oh yes," she said. "It certainly was. I believe you and your master were the last to visit me. The methods of locating the center of my sphere change on a regular basis. Since Okami, many have attempted to find me. Very few make it to the sphere in this desert. Of the few that have, all have perished before making it to the third room."

"Have any of The Dark Men attempted to find you?" Cosden asked her.

"Of that I am certain. And of their failure to do so, I am also certain."

"Is there anything else you need to tell me?" Cosden asked.

"There is much I need to tell you," she said.

"And what is that?" Cosden asked.

"I'm afraid you must ask the question before I can form the answer."

"Alright then," he said. "I'm trying to think."

"I have a question," said The Professor. "That might help prod Cosden along."

"Wonderful," The Map Maker smiled.

"What do you have mapped out in this room?" The Professor asked.

"Everything."

"Everything?" The Professor asked. "Everything on earth?"

The Map Maker chuckled. Then she walked over to a large stack of papers and pulled out several rolls of parchment. She spread the paper onto her desk and revealed drawings of constellations, earthly states, oceans, and countless geometric shapes that Cosden was not familiar with.

"I document far more than what is within the bounds of this planet," she said. "Of course, I document everything here as well."

"What does that mean?" Cosden asked.

"Every ocean, every landmark, every mountain, every epeirogenic deformation and every orogenic formation. I have documented it all since Earth's creation. It's all here in this room."

"But you said you documented everything beyond Earth as well," Cosden said.

"Yes," she answered. "The accumulation of all celestial bodies, the formation of each solar system, and the beginning and death of every star located on the main sequence. I have charted it all—in this room. That is my job."

"But I'm not here for that," Cosden told her. "What you do is quite a service to the universe. Just as The Time Keeper looks over time and space, you chart it. But I am here for specific information regarding very specific men."

"We will need to take a step back," she said. "Let's move away from the celestial and toward the earthly."

The Map Maker grabbed the numerous maps and papers from her desk and shoved it into an old filing cabinet in one of the corners of the small room.

"I know it may not seem like much," she told them, "but these cabinets are quite deep. Each one holds a few billion years of information."

She opened another cabinet and reached deep inside of it. She pulled out a stack of hundreds of papers and plopped them right on her desk. Then she divided the single stack into three small stacks.

"You are searching for the present, correct?" she asked.

"Yes," Cosden answered.

"Perfect. I suspected as much. What are the specifics?"

"We are searching for a man. Or many, in fact. Do you have information on people?"

"Yes," she said. "I apologize for not making it more readily apparent. Just as I collect information for the infinite, I, too, collect for the finite."

"But we're not just looking for any person," Cosden told her. "We're seeking The Dark Men."

"Oh, that might be a tough one," she said as she tapped her finger against the desk. "Let's see what I have."

She opened another cabinet and pulled out yet another stack of papers. These papers were old, dusty, and appeared to have been untouched for thousands of years.

"It should be here," The Map Maker said as she placed the stack of papers on the available portion of her desk. She flipped through countless pages.

"I'm afraid I can provide little information about them. As The Map Maker, I know only their whereabouts."

"That's all I'm searching for," Cosden said.

"The Dark Men take many forms. But their personification in the singularity can be readily found," The Map Maker said as she flipped through page after page. Then she grabbed a red quill pen from a cup that lied on her desk and circled a marking upon an elaborate dusty map.

"Here," she pointed to the circled marking.

"Where is this?" Cosden asked.

"The terminal of The Grand Union Station of Atlanta, Georgia," The Map Maker answered. "Southern United

States."

"That's impossible," said The Professor.

"Why?" asked The Map Maker.

"Because The Union Station of Atlanta was demolished in 1972."

"But there it is, on my map," she told him.

"Is it possible your map is outdated?" Cosden asked.

"No," she answered. "They update themselves. My maps are never wrong."

"Then how do you explain this?" Kokoro asked.

"It is not obvious?" asked The Map Maker.

"I believe I understand," said Cosden. "If your maps are never wrong, then the Union Station is alive and well in the city of Atlanta. But it can only be seen by those who need to see it."

"That way," The Professor theorized, "the Dark Men can conduct business without interruption. By rebuilding a terminal no one else can see."

"Exactly," said The Map Maker. "That's where you'll find him."

"What do you mean 'him'?" The Professor asked her.

"Their singularity of perception."

"The one I encountered in Nazi Germany?" Cosden asked.

"Yes," Kokoro told him. "That's the one."

"No," Cosden said. "No, no, no. That's not enough! That can't be it."

"What else do you seek?" The Map Maker asked.

"I need all of them," Cosden said. "All of them together in one place—just one of them won't do. I need to know where all of The Dark Men gather at once. It's the only way to get rid of them."

"I'll see what I can find," said The Map Maker.

She flipped through the same stack of papers until she

found another sheet of paper buried halfway through the stack. The piece of paper was as old as the others but couldn't be deciphered. The paper was covered in inkblots and smears.

"I've never seen this before," The Map Maker told them.

"What is it?" Cosden asked.

"This parchment should divulge the location of their gathering spot. But it's indecipherable—completely."

"They've clouded their location," Cosden said.

"For obvious reasons," The Professor scoffed. "Now you see the power they wield. To obfuscate the maps of one of the universe's most loyal interpreters."

"Regardless," said The Map Maker, "as long as you know their most secretive destination, then you should be able to locate their gathering location."

"The Map Maker is right," The Professor confirmed. "They desire Cosden. In order to control him at his current exceeding rate of abilities, it will require their power in vast numbers—likely all of them."

"That's when I'll strike," said Cosden. When they're all together."

"We," Kokoro clarified. "That's when we'll strike."

"We'll be right by your side," said The Professor.

Cosden looked to Hosuto.

"I said that I would guide you here and you promised me I would then be free," said Hosuto.

"That's correct," Cosden told him. "You are free to go whenever you like."

"You have proven yourself a worthy successor to Okami," said Hosuto. "I stand before you and admit with full confidence that you are the begetter. If there is a war to be fought, I shall be by your side."

"Not as a servant," Cosden bowed his head to him, "but as an equal."

"Battle will commence at the terminal," Hosuto said with confidence. "With each of us by your side."

"Then it is settled," Cosden told them. "We will travel to the Union Station and find the Dark Men—immediately."

"Wait," said The Map Maker, her arm outstretched as if to stop Cosden.

"What is it?" Cosden asked.

"Minutes ago I told you that I could not help you beyond the locations listed upon my maps."

"Yes."

"But that is not the truth. I told you only what you needed to know when you needed to know it. But now that you are seeking to clash with the Dark Men, there is further information that may be of use to you."

"What kind of information?" he asked.

"Wisdom. Understanding. Perspective. At least in possibility," she answered.

"Go on."

The Map Maker grabbed a small key from her pocket and strolled over to another filing cabinet. She unlocked the bottom drawer of the cabinet and pulled out a small pamphlet wrapped in string.

"Here," she said, handing the tattered booklet to Cosden.

"What is this?" Cosden asked.

"You asked me if any of The Dark Men attempted to penetrate the walls of this sphere. I told you yes. Many years ago, three of them arrived in police uniforms."

"Their usual attire," The Professor interjected.

"They were powerful but not powerful enough. They perished in the third room. But they left behind something— that booklet. It reads like a narrative, perhaps a manifesto. I have kept it hidden with the intentions of sharing it only with you."

"What's it about?" Cosden asked her.

"It is set only decades ago. I know not if it is the authentic beginning of The Dark Men but it is a necessary read if you wish to know them—or him. According to that work, The Dark Men were once one. At any rate, I have taken to referencing it as 'The Book of John' and perhaps it is best if you read it for yourself."

"Thank you."

He unwrapped the string around the booklet and began reading—

THE BOOK OF JOHN

Around the turn of the second millennium, there lived John. He was a teenager (skinny, pale) who lived with his father in one of his city's worst neighborhoods. He was bullied, and beaten just as often. Something had to be done—something had to change. He became obsessed with change so much that his dream was to change the world. That would eventually happen—he would change the world quite literally. But first it is important to know the context for why this change occurred.

Life for John began with his mother and father. He was optimistic like any child. But as the years wore on, things changed drastically. John's father was a decorated veteran of war. The records he set during war were as innumerable as the medals he received for his bravery and sacrifice. But years later, the veteran father returned home a different man. He lost a limb—his left leg, in the war and trauma ravaged him.

"Your father's not feeling well," John's mother often told him.

"What's wrong?" 13-year-old John asked.

"Woke up sweating. Forgot he was home."

"Has he been drinking?" John asked.

"Yes," his mother answered. "It's the only thing that helps."

"It doesn't help!" John shouted. "It makes things worse."

His mother grabbed him. She held him tight. It was the only embrace that made John feel whole.

"It's going to be okay," she told him as she often did.

Eventually, things worsened for John. He lost his only steady rock. But it was a gradual decline. One day as John's father was drinking, his mother ran into the street. She narrowly missed being hit by a car. John panicked as he brought her back into the house and questioned her intentions.

"I saw a light," his mother told him.

"What?" John asked with shock.

He could make little sense of what she told him.

"I was looking for the light. The brightest light," she cried.

"What does that mean?" he asked again.

She never gave him an answer and John relegated the incident to a mere lapse in judgement. But days later her speech was disorganized. She spoke words in random orders as the father, who rarely left the house, continued drinking.

"I don't understand what you're saying, mom."

"I've got to find the light. It's coming I won't."

"Find got I've to light," she said.

"What!?"

"Run and me for won't it's coming I."

John was left as disoriented as his mother's speech. He had no one to turn to. His father listened to nothing. His friends were non-existent. Authority figures in his life were unhelpful, and he couldn't bear the embarrassment of having both a mother and a father who were unable to properly function in everyday life. The following week she refused to speak at all.

"Mom, why won't you talk?"

Catatonic, she refused to speak. She looked in her son's direction with dead eyes that peered right past him.

"No use," his father slurred.

"What?" John asked.

"She ain't talkin' to no one. Not me, not you."

"What's wrong with her?"

"What do you mean, John?" he slurred. "She's a dingbat. That's who I married."

"Don't say that about her!"

"Just look at her for yerself, Johnny," he belched and extended an arm out in her direction. "She's completely lost it. And she ain't ever been to war. Imagine what that'd do to 'er," he laughed drunkenly.

"Why are you even here!?" John yelled.

His father clenched his teeth, slapped John in the face, and shoved him against a wall. "You live in my home, boy."

That was the first time John had cried in years.

The mother's condition got worse. She was plagued by hallucinations, delusions, and emotional emptiness toward her husband and son. It devastated John. It destroyed his spirits. But he refused to give up and refused to allow himself to think that life couldn't improve. While the father sat in the living room, drunken and asleep, John lied with his mother in bed each night.

"We're going to get you to a doctor tomorrow, mom. You're going to be okay."

She said nothing.

"Remember when we'd go to the lake?" John said. "We'll do that again real soon when you get better. I promise."

Then she spoke for the first time in weeks. "I've got to go, John."

"What?"

He couldn't believe she was speaking again.

"The light is calling me," she said. "I have to find it."

"Mother, what are you talking about?"

"I have to find it, John! I have to go where the light grows brighter."

"There's no light coming after you, mother. You have to trust me. You're seeing things."

"No," she demanded. "It's real. I know it's real. The light controls everything. Now it's after me. It won't stop. The light is the second key."

"Key to what?" he asked her.

"The key to the universe. It's summoning me, John. It wants me."

She stood up from her bed, peering around as John pulled her back down. He held her, rocking with her as she cried over what she deemed "the light." He comforted her as best as he could and eventually she fell asleep. The disarray was over, at least for the night.

"Mom!" John called out the next morning as he exited his old home. "I'm leaving for class! See you in the morning."

"Get out of here!" his father yelled at him from the living room sofa. "She'll have a nice bottle of pills to keep her head screwed on when you get back."

While John headed off to school, it was the role of his father to take the mother for a proper check-up that day. Her appointment was scheduled for ten in the morning. But as the morning hours passed, the father fell into a deep sleep, aided by handful of alcoholic beverages.

John's mother awoke that morning in a panic. She knew the light was searching for her as she jumped out of bed and dressed herself.

"Doctor," the father slurred, half asleep. "Half… hour…"

"I've got to go," said the mother, speaking only to herself. "The light is moving faster and faster. It's growing."

"Shuddup," the father slurred with one eye shut. "I'm tryin' ta' sleep."

"Must leave now," the mother said to herself. "Can't wait."

The father was now fast asleep as a beer bottel rolled from

his loose fingers. The mother's car had been sold only a month prior. While driving, she ran into a parking meter, a fire hydrant, and a mailbox. That was when the family realized she had no business behind the wheel of a car. So now that she intended to leave the house in order to search for "the light," she needed a car in which to travel.

"Keys," she said to herself. "Need keys."

She tore her bedroom apart, searching for car keys.

"Where are they!?"

She headed to the living room where the husband slept.

"Where are the keys!?" she yelled at him. Raising her voice did not awaken him from a stupor—it never did.

She searched under the cushions of the sofa and behind the old television set that rarely showed more than static.

"Must be somewhere," she said in a panicked manner. Then she came upon a realization. Her husband had car keys.

"Honey, where are your keys?" she whispered.

When he remained asleep, she dove her hand straight into the pockets of his ratty tattered bathroom. There she found it—a set of jingling, shimmering keys to the old truck outside.

"The light," she rattled off. "The light. The light."

She ran out of the house and hopped into the car. The ignition took several attempts before successfully starting. The old truck she took had been in her husband's possession for many years—bought before he was ever a serviceman. Then she placed the car in reversed, pulled onto the street, and sped off.

The light in her mind turned to voices and the voices began to call her. The same voices steered her through the streets.

"The light," she muttered over and over.

She hit lampposts, drove over lawns, ran into stop signs,

and continued driving.

"Old as time," she said to herself. "Follow the light to find the creator."

She drove uninterrupted for over twenty minutes, accelerating at every intersection.

"Here," she said as she parked in front of a train station. "The light is here... The light is here."

She shut off the truck, jumped out, and ran toward the terminal. She peered inside and spotted dozens of individuals, both standing and sitting.

"Too many people," she said. "They'll stop me. They'll stop me from meeting the light."

Quickly, she shut the door of the terminal and removed her shoes. With bare feet she ran around the back of the terminal. There were six other people sitting across benches, waiting for the train to arrive.

"They're shutting this station down," said one of the sitting men. "Only a few more rides will ever pass through this station."

"Sign of the times," said the woman next to him as she flipped through her newspaper.

"This station is almost as old as the city," the man spoke again. Then he checked his wristwatch.

"Shutting down," John's mother repeated to herself. "The light is leaving. No... it can't. Have to catch it before too late."

Speeding to the back of the building had tired her out. She was sweating, hair flopping in every direction, and now bare feet. Her feet were even bleeding from the rocks on which she stepped. But to her, that mattered nothing.

"Can't let the light leave without me."

She removed her necklace and dropped it on the ground. Then she looked to the outdoor clock, installed for commuters. A loud horn sounded through the air. It was the steam engine of the train growing near.

"The light!" she said desperately.

At the front of the locomotive was a bright luminous light.

"There… the light," she spoke catatonically. "The light… The beginning…"

The train drew near and John's mother walked to the edge of terminal's ledge.

"Hey lady, be careful!" a man said. "Get back! You could fall."

"Are you okay, miss?" a woman asked. "Don't get too close to the ledge."

The train drew closer.

"7… 6… 5… 4…" she counted.

Finally someone stood up from the bench. But before they could reach John's mother, she finished her countdown. Just as the train swept into the station, she threw herself onto the tracks. Every witness screamed in terror. The bright light was the only thing the mother saw. It was the last thing she saw. Then everything went black.

———

John was called into the principal's office at noon. Standing next to the principal was his father, whose tattered outfit reeked of the whisky he drank that morning.

"She's gone," the father said bluntly.

"I'm so sorry," the principal parroted.

"What?" was all John could ask.

"Your mother's gone," the father belched. "Took 'er life this mornin' after you went to class."

For a moment, the only thing young John could hear was his own heartbeat.

"No," John said with denial. "That's a lie. You took her to

the doctor this morning."

"Sorry," the father said. "I didn't. Fell asleep. Woke up and my keys were missing. Got a call an hour later."

"How could you?" John asked him, his voice a mere tremble. "I trusted you… She was supposed to get better."

"She's 'n a better place now… That's all I can think of, Johnny."

"No… no… no… no… no," was all the boy could say.

"She finally found that light she was lookin' for. Sorry, kid," the father hawked.

"I hate you."

Those were the last words John spoke to his father for a full month. For the first week, John ran away. He was discovered by officers who delivered him to his father. He spent the next several weeks in a state of selective mutism. All he could do was replay in his head the last night he spent with his mother. *What was so important about the light?*

The father continued to drink and the state of his and John's stability collapsed further. The father's habits became worse as he replaced the drinks with other substances. The sofa became his permanent home, as he lay on it all day and all night—rarely speaking, even to his own son. As the months passed and the year came to a close, the state of their house was near dilapidation.

John still preferred to not speak to his father, but he eventually rebounded from both his mutism and constant state of depression. But mostly, he learned to become more independent than ever. That was a necessity.

"Going to school, old man," he told his father in the morning before class.

"Uh… uh-huh… yea…" was the most his father could slur through in the morning.

John even made a friend as he entered high school. With the closing of the high school closest to his house, he was bused to a much nicer area. An area whose population he had never interacted with. They were children whose parents had money, cars, nice clothing. So John didn't fit in. But he found a kindred spirit one day in another boy named Charles.

"You've got your own car?" John asked him in astonishment.

"Yeah," Charles said, as if owning a car were akin to owning shoes. "Dad bought me two actually."

In fact, Charles was likely the wealthiest student at the school. And here he was, hanging out with the poorest.

"Is there anything you don't have?"

"Got everything I've ever wanted," Charles told him. "You don't?"

"Not really," John answered modestly, without telling him the full extent of his circumstances.

But eventually, John would open up to his new friend. He explained to him the situation with his father and deceased mother. He explained why his clothing was old and why his stringy mop of blonde hair had not been cut in over a year.

"I could totally help you out," Charles told him on more than one occasion.

But John refused. He didn't want gifts or money or charity. But Charles pleaded so often and so hard that John eventually relented. Charles purchased him clothes and drove him to school each morning. "Because that's what friends are for."

When John's father was too much for him to deal with, he'd stay at his new friend's house. It was palatial. Three stories high, spotless floors, and a game room. John knew he had been born in the wrong family, but he was happy to be friends with the right one.

Eventually, John met other friends of Charles. There was Clark, a quarterback. Sarah, a cheerleader. Chloe, smartest kid on campus. Andrew, coolest kid on campus.

But Charles didn't connect with them. He didn't understand them and they surely didn't understand him. Most of the school continued to think of him as weird, odd, and unfit for their school. John paid little attention to what others had to say about him. He preferred to remain outside of their social circles and cared for none of them but Charles.

"You've gotta get along with some of them!" Charles told him on the way to school one morning.

"Nope," John answered. "Not really. Just you."

"Come on, John! You've just got to know them a little more like you know me. I bet you didn't like me at first either."

"I guess that's true."

"Remember Clark?"

"The football player?"

"Yeah. He's putting together a huge party this weekend. I wanted to invite you. It'll give you a chance to meet some cool people, right?"

"They probably don't want me there," John said bashfully.

"No way, they're cool with you. You gotta be there."

"Sure," John agreed. "Sounds fun."

That weekend, John attended the party at his friend's request. It was an outdoor get together with loud music, beer, and more students than John had ever seen gathered in one area. He stood away from the others and kept to himself. Every few minutes a group of kids would pass by him and point out "the weird kid." He was the only one who wouldn't socialize at a party. A few girls approached him but their social demeanors disinterested him. So he stood alone, not speaking to anyone, for an hour. He looked around and could find Charles nowhere.

"John, over here!"

He looked up and spotted his only friend.

"John, come with me!"

"What… Why?"

"We found something, you've gotta see this!"

"See what?" John asked.

"Down the road. There's this old abandoned barn out there."

"Yeah?"

"You gotta check it out. There's something inside. Come on!"

Uninterested, John reluctantly followed his friend. They raced away from the party, across the tracks, and onto the other side of the street. There they came across the old barn.

"I don't see what's so special about an old barn that no one uses," John said.

"It's what's inside the barn!" Charles told him. "Come on!"

They dashed to the back of the barn and walked in through the exit door. Inside the barn were six other students including the football player, the cheerleader, the school's smartest girl, and the school's coolest guy. But what really mattered was the object located in the middle of the barn—a giant crystal that reached the top of the barn itself. It was dimly glowing in every color of the rainbow spectrum.

"What is this?" John asked.

"No clue," said Clark, the football player. "I've never seen anything like it."

"What should we do?" Charles asked them.

"Touch it," John said, enraptured by the giant object.

"You first," Charles told him.

"How about all together?" said Clark.

The seven all nodded. They reached out and placed their hands upon the crystal. Its colors flashed bright and faster. Then everything went dark.

John awoke the next morning in his bedroom. He had no

recollection of how he got home; he only knew the feeling of a headache from jumping out of bed too quickly. But that wasn't normal. He lay back down, shut his eyes for several moments, and then got out of bed for the second time.

Objects began whizzing through the air—socks, shirts, boxes. Then John realized that these objects were being controlled by his mind. He had been granted telekinetic abilities. And so had the other seven students who touched the crystal. They could move objects by thought and command them in every direction. These incredible powers brought John closer to his peers. They spent countless weekends together honing their skills to a level of mastery.

One night, while walking along railroad tracks, they watched a train derail. They came to its rescue, saving countless lives in the process. That was the moment they decided to use their abilities to benefit others.

"We could be like superheroes, maybe?" Clark suggested.

And that was what they did—at first. For a few months they worked together, united as partners for a positive cause. But strife soon set in.

"I thought I was in charge here!?" Clark questioned them.

"No way," Charles would shout back. "This is a team effort."

They fought and slammed objects into one another. Some became too involved while others became disinterested. That was when they decided to part ways. One night, right before everyone decided to go their separate ways, one of the boys got into a petty argument with John. The argument turned into a fight and led to the boy's accidental death. John was alone and afraid. He had not meant for the boy to die. But something else happened—the spirit of the crystal left the boy's body and entered John. It changed him. He felt stronger and more powerful than ever before.

And then he left his body. His spirit flew through the

cosmos and revealed to him the world as it really is. He understood that every object and every person in his life was an illusion. And even he was an illusion—all projections of the begetter, the only true soul in existence. But he knew how to change it. The crystal he touched that fateful night was a piece of the begetter's fractal palace. For every portion of it he consumed, the more conscious he would become. Until finally, his soul would exist just as the begetter's soul existed.

With his head swirling with more thoughts than he could control, he went home that night.

"Where've you been!?" he father yelled after waking. He stood up and faced John.

"I was out," John said calmly. "Now get out of my face."

His father inched closer to him. "I'll do whatever I damn well please. Look at you. What kind of future have you got?"

"Have you taken a look at yourself?" John asked him angrily.

"I lived my life, boy. You see those medals. You see where my leg used to be! I paid my debt. Then I got stuck with that miserable woman you called a mother. I'm half glad she's gone."

"You insignificant, pathetic man. You don't really exist, you know that?"

He slapped John in the face. And in return, John threw him against the wall without effort. Lying on the floor, covered in debris, his father coughed and was unable to pick himself up. He clenched his heart and died only seconds later. Then tears filled John's eyes.

"What have I done?"

"You've done only what you need to do," a soft voice called out.

John looked up and discovered the luminous spirit of his mother.

"Mother?" he said, trembling.

"You have unlocked an unimaginable portion of the universe," the phantasm told him. "The light of the sustainer came for me. It will seek you out and you must be ready. Just as it found me at the train station, so shall it find you in the same location—one day. You must be prepared."

"What do I do?" he begged.

"You must consume the power of the sustainer. You have but a small piece. When you have all pieces, so shall you be conscious of the universe. So shall you control the skies and the earth and the factors time, just as the sustainer does. He will attempt to destroy you. But if you subjugate him first, you may suppress his consciousness. Then and only then will you be ruler of all there is and all there ever will be."

"What must I do?" John asked his mother as he fell to his knees.

"You must eliminate your peers. The powers of the fractal were split between each of you. Those fragments must be whole. You must kill them. Clark, Sarah, Chloe, even Charles."

"No," John cried. "Charles is my friend. My only friend."

"It is the only way to absorb the light they hold," the phantasm of his mother told him. "It is the only way to equip yourself against the sustainer. He cannot be destroyed entirely, least the universe itself be destroyed. But he can be suppressed. God's power can be your power."

"I'm not strong enough," John cried. "I can't kill anyone!"

"What have you done tonight but killed two?" she asked him. "If it is a sign you want, look no further than those bodies. You must kill all who stand in your way. And what are they but creations of the sustainer? I have shown you the path to power. Only you can take it. Become the authority of the universe."

"Yes, mother," he cried. "Just don't leave me."

"I will be with you always," she said softly.

John blew through the roof and flew through the sky—a power he acquired after killing the first boy. Next he would take the keys to time, space, life, control, and infinite power. Power corrupted him, engrossed him, and tormented him.

First to go were the two lesser-known boys who held powers from the crystal, Andrew and Daniel. The two juniors from his school were gathered with other friends at a party when John ripped the door from its hinges. The house shook as teenagers ran away screaming as John killed everyone in his path.

Andrew and Daniel attempted to fight back, but they were little match for John. When their bodies lied lifeless, John consumed the light they emitted. He now held the power of four—his eyes, the tint of rage.

The next to go were the football player, Clark and the cheerleader, Sarah—then two others whom John cared nothing about. Their death was a means to an end—a necessity to ensuring the survival of order within the universe.

"I know what you've done, John," Charles said when they finally met for the last time.

"But do you know why?" John asked.

"There's no explanation you can provide for killing all of your friends!" Charles yelled.

"My friends?" John scoffed. "They mean nothing to me, Charles."

"What about me, John? What do I mean to you?"

"That's why this won't be easy for me. But I have a destiny to fulfill. The world depends on it. I don't want to, Charles. But I have to."

"You to have to, what, John? Kill me?"

"I need what you hold, Charles."

Charles placed his hand over his chest and pulled from

within him a glowing orb. He walked closer to John and placed it in his hand.

"Have it," Charles said, his eyes filled with tears at the thought of his lost ones.

"After my mother died, I never thought I would be accepted by anyone," John told him. "Then you showed up. I won't forget you, Charles."

John absorbed the contents of the orb into the palm of his hand and shot into the air. It was the last time he would ever see Charles. But now, with the full power of the fractal crystal, John wielded immeasurable power. Though limited only to a few centuries in reach, he could travel through time, insert himself at any interval as a conqueror and the authority of all servility.

"There is no rate at which to halt my abilities," he once said. "For I will be controller of all."

He split himself up into countless figures of authority, whom all would obey. Each figure was stationed at every period of time within the existence of the human race. He would bring order to the orderless and contain the chaos of the universe.

Splitting himself into countless pieces required immense power. It required his conscious to be split up for the countless bodies he wished to inhabit. Eventually, he inhabited so many selves that the physical self lost distinction. Each new figure became faceless and featureless. The many faces came only in the form of false projection, given to the authority figures who now dressed in uniforms and patrolled humanity—The Dark Men.

But the original manifestation remained—the adult version of John. The visions of his mother continued to visit him, until he wished for her no more. Then he spoke only to himself.

"Why would I need to converse with human projections

that don't exist? What use have they but subjugation in the maintenance of order?" asked the main manifestation.

"Do you feel it?" a faceless officer of his own conscious asked. "The sustainer grows stronger. His physical form grows and gains while we... lose."

"If we can suppress his knowledge, we can suppress his capacity. But it's different this time. He has left for himself a series of personifications. Knowledge, time, space, volition. If the sustainer is reaches each personification, he will control everything."

"But we've yet to figure how to exist without him."

"That would require our transmigration from this universe to another."

"One that is all our own."

"Until then, we must seize control of Cosden Ke. He's too powerful to be left alone."

•••

"And that was the Book of John," The Map Maker said as Cosden closed the booklet he had just read.

"So that is his beginning?" Cosden asked The Map Maker.

"Its validity cannot be determined by me," she said to him.

"It is a fascinating story," said The Professor. "We should be sure to keep an open mind."

"Thank you," Cosden told her. "I hope that perhaps we can find some use for this. But now we've got to get to Union Station."

"Just one more thing," The Map Maker told him.

Cosden faced her as an orb materialized in the palm of her hand.

"This," she said, "is how you will reach me. Immediately and directly."

"No more puzzle rooms," Hosuto said.

"Never again," The Map Maker smiled. "And that there is just as good for exits."

She handed the glowing orb to Cosden and watched as it dematerialized into his own palm.

"Good luck," she wished him.

Cosden smiled, closed his eyes, and made himself and everyone around him teleport through space and time. They were instantaneously removed from The Map Maker's sphere to a sunny deserted area back within the borders of the United States.

"Where are we?" Kokoro asked him.

"Atlanta, Georgia, USA. This is as close as I could get to the destination on The Map Maker's most helpful map. The Dark Men cloud the area, making it impossible to teleport to their precise location."

"But it can't be far from here," The Professor reminded him.

"I suppose that is comforting," Cosden nodded.

"So the plan is to find the main manifestation," said Hosuto. "Then allow him to draw all of The Dark Men near. Then you defeat them."

"Sounds relatively easy, does it not?" Cosden said nonchalantly.

"We'd better be on our way," The Professor reminded them.

"Completely," Cosden agreed.

They walked down the path of an empty street with only trees and sunny skies in view.

"What part of town are we in?" Kokoro asked.

"The outskirts, clearly," Cosden answered. "We could apparate no closer, I'm afraid."

"So we'll have quite a walk," she asked him.

"Let us hope not. Mere minutes could hold the key to the

fate of our world."

Hosuto stopped. "Wait," he whispered to the others. They turned to face him and stopped in their tracks.

"What is it?" Kokoro asked.

"Did you not hear that?" Hosuto asked, peering around their environment.

"Hear what?" The Professor asked.

"The bushes," said Hosuto. "The bushes just lightly brushed in the opposite direction of the wind."

"I think he's right," Cosden said.

"It is a sound most distinct," Hosuto whispered. Then he pulled out his sword. "Quiet."

"Can we proceed?" Kokoro asked.

"Cautiously," Cosden nodded.

They continued walking while Hosuto took slow deliberate steps behind the rest of them. His eyes darted from left to right as his ears picked up the smallest sound of an unnatural occurrence within the trees around them.

"I think it's safe now," The Professor said.

Suddenly a faceless uniformed officer with two blades extending from his arms leapt out of the bushes. Hosuto was the first to react, when he raised his sword into the air and sliced the faceless officer the moment the ominous figure's feet touched the ground.

"Or perhaps not," said The Professor again.

Cosden extended his arm out and from his palm exerted a small lightning bolt. The bolt connected with the faceless figure and dematerialized him into a million particles that floated away.

"You see how that works," Cosden told them. "Even when broken down to its molecular structure, it merely floats away to join a stronger self."

"That is why they must all be destroyed at once," said Kokoro.

"By the way," Cosden said. "Thank you, Hosuto."

"I am privileged to please the begetter and serve as his enforcement."

"I see why Okami kept you near," Cosden smiled faintly. "Let's press on."

"Are you sure each decision you make is the correct one?" Kokoro asked him.

"I believe so," Cosden answered as they walked for another mile. "I believe myself to be capable of making only one decision—the one I go with. Sure, there are alternate paths and choices presented to me. But they don't constitute a decision unless I actually move forward with it."

"So how do you know if the option you take is the correct one?" she asked.

"I do not. If the choice I make is in the incorrect one—if it is one that leads to suffering, to torment, then I assume it is the path I was meant to take. Or else I would not be taking it in the first place."

"And for the first time," Kokoro told him. "I must humbly disagree."

"Feel free," Cosden said. "But tell me why?"

"Because I do not believe choices to be so static. Choices can be redone, paths can be retaken. It is not a necessity to endure a path of great resistance and struggle just because your original choice lied in a folly decision. That original choice can be altered and shifted to reach a more harmonious path. So as I said, I do not believe choice to be static."

"Perhaps my mind is still quite grounded in the world in which I grew up," Cosden smiled. "Because such a stance is not what I'm familiar with."

She returned his smile with one of her own. "But what better way to form a more accordant subsistence than to make positive alterations to the familiarity."

"I cannot disagree," he said.

"Just keep this view near. You never know when it may come in handy."

"I shall."

"And most of all," Kokoro said, "I think it's what The Clinician would want."

"Professor," Cosden turned his head. "Do you have anything you'd like to add to this dialogue?"

"No, no," The Professor smiled. "I'm most pleased to be a mere spectator for now."

"A mere spectator?" Cosden asked.

"Yes."

"Professor," Cosden said as he locked his hands together while they continued their path, "there is nothing *mere* about being a spectator. An astute observer is capable of learning an extraordinary, if not unequalled, measure."

"Ah, so they are," The Professor smiled.

"Although," Cosden said. "Because you are a personification, I am unsure if you are capable of learning more than what you already know—to be frank."

"An honest inquiry," The Professor told him. "One I have wondered quite often."

"And what conclusion have you arrived at? If you don't mind me asking, Professor."

"Ask away!" he said. "I've concluded that my fixed allocation, as just one of your many personifications, does not stifle an ability to learn or grow. I can learn from you just as you from me. And I am proud to have done just that over the course of this journey."

"I'm glad to hear," Cosden nodded.

"And I'm sure you've learned at least a little," The Professor chuckled.

After another mile of walking, there remained little in sight besides the concrete road and the tall trees surrounding the path.

"Are we sure this is the right path?" Kokoro asked.

"It is still noon," Hosuto said. "We shall walk until the sun lowers beneath our vantage point if we must."

"That's quite a spirit there, Hosuto," The Professor joked. "Quite the opposite of how you felt within The Map Maker's sphere."

"But here I remain," Hosuto said. "Just as Master Ke has proven himself on many occasions, so shall I prove my loyalty."

"Have you thought about what comes next?" Kokoro asked Cosden.

"What do you mean?"

"What lies ahead—beyond The Dark Men. Where harmony lies."

"No," Cosden answered. "I haven't thought about it."

"Neither have I," Kokoro admitted.

"I can't exactly return to a college life with my roommate, can I? He was one of them after all… I threw him out of a window, you know."

Kokoro laughed. "I am familiar. But I remain serious in my inquiry."

"I truly don't know," Cosden answered. "If you were the begetter of the universe, at least according to your friends, how would you spend the remainder of eternity?"

"I think that is a question most impossible to answer," said Kokoro.

"Ah," Cosden smiled. "Now you understand my perspective."

"Even as the creator?"

"Particularly as the creator. But there's something more overwhelming. I recently began to remember."

"Remember what?" she asked.

"Everything—but only in fragments. I can recall the beginning, the creation. I can recall the formation of the universe as if I were there. But it feels stranger than usual. It feels like what I would call second-hand images. As if the images aren't mine to begin with, but were passed down to me as memories."

"I imagine those images will grow stronger with time," The Professor told him. "I'm most certain of it."

"The Map Maker has drawn out my path—my journey, since the beginning. And according to her, I have come in other forms."

"Yes," said The Professor.

"But does that not contradict the notion that nothing came before me? If 'me' is something that simply takes countless forms over the history of our beginnings. Is this body merely a vessel? Or will I occupy it until the end of times?"

"If you are the begetter then I imagine it is up to you," The Professor told him. "But perhaps that is a conversation best suited for another personification."

"The Clinician?" Cosden asked.

"Perhaps."

"Up ahead!" yelled Hosuto.

In the distance was a train station.

"I believe that's it!" Cosden.

"I thought we'd never reach it," Kokoro said with a huge relief.

"Careful," The Professor warned them. "We don't know precisely what's there."

"We know exactly who's there!" Hosuto said.

"But do we know how many?" The Professor asked. "Could be one or one million. Do not underestimate The Dark Men."

They walked closer and closer as the large train station came into a more flourished view. Tracks lay around it and the terminal's top was made of stainless glass. The rest was spotless red brick. It was quite a sight—the most elaborate and vast train station imaginable.

Standing directly in front of the train station's entrance was a figure that became clearer the closer they walked toward him. Finally, as reached a speaking distance, Cosden could make out precisely who it was—the main personification of The Dark Men. He had the same face as he had in Nazi-occupied France and wore a dark officer's uniform that Cosden had come to fully associate with them.

"Shhh," the pale man said as he placed his index finger to his lips.

The sun itself began to rapidly shift. It quickly lowered from the sun as darkness engulfed everything.

"When did you learn to do that?" Cosden asked.

The pale figure smiled. "You liked that one, did you?"

"How many of you are here?" Cosden asked.

"Just me," he spoke with faint laughter.

"You sure about that?"

"Why don't you drop in and find out, Cosden?"

The double doors of the train station opened.

"I don't trust him," Hosuto whispered.

"I wouldn't trust me either," The Dark Man chuckled. "Can't blame you."

"You want us to join you? In there?" Cosden asked.

"Come on," he replied. "We'll just have a chat."

Cosden looked to The Professor, he looked to Kokoro, and then he turned back to The Dark Man.

"What have I to lose?" Cosden asked.

The Dark Man turned around and walked through the doors of the train station. Cosden, The Professor, Kokoro, and Hosuto all followed.

It was empty inside—in addition to cold and pristine. The Dark Man faced them, his hands by his side. His voice echoed as he yelled, "Home sweet home!

"Right, Cosden?" he spoke again.

"That's the second time you've called me Cosden."

"That's correct. And this would be the third time, Cosden. That is your name, is it not? There's something about it. It's somewhat peculiar. Somewhat fascinating. Odd yet strangely fitting. Almost as if it were symbolic or meaningful, or maybe not. It stands out but not enough to warrant much attention. Just like the rest of you."

"If you are to call me Cosden, does that mean I can refer to you as John?"

The Dark Man's face subtly twisted in annoyance as Cosden spoke again.

"John? Can I use that name?"

Finally The Dark Man spoke up.

"John?" he sniveled. "Have you read—"

"The little book? Yes. I have. We all have."

"Funny little story, isn't it, Cosden?"

"If you say so. I personally found it more sad than funny. Rather tragic even."

"Is that meant to get under my skin, Cosden?"

"Not at all. I'm merely reflecting on the story you presumably wrote. I felt sorry for John."

"Why, Cosden? Did he come across as forlorn, defenseless, feeble to you?"

"I would describe him as helpless."

"Helpless?" The Dark Man asked.

"And intensely sad," Cosden added. "He was powerless and unloved. Those are strong feelings, particularly for a young man in search of himself. But then he thought he found it—power, that is. The anger never subsided. He wished for nothing more than authoritarian control, wouldn't you say?"

The Dark Man said nothing for a moment. Then spoke. "Are you sure about that, Cosden? Are you sure that's what he wanted?"

"Over the last few minutes, I have picked up your penchant for referring to John as he. Shouldn't you refer to him as *I*? Or are you so removed from that young man, in your quest for universal transmogrification, that you are him no longer?"

"A fascinating theory, Cosden. But how can you be so sure? How do you *know* that story is mine? How do you *know* it is authentic? What if I told you that is but one of many storied pasts floating around. How would you know which one is correct?"

"I wouldn't know."

"Precisely, Cosden."

"But I wouldn't need to know. Sometimes one can simply trust their way to the truth. And in this case, I trust 'The Book of John' to be true."

"'The Book of John?'" he laughed. "Is that what you've dubbed it?"

"It's what The Map Maker named it. I found it to be quite apt."

"Regardless, Mister Ke."

"Do she still visit you?"

"Does she visit me?" The Dark Man repeated with confusion.

"Your mother. Her apparition."

"I've told you, you've read a work of fiction, Mister Ke."

"Are you sure about that, John? Was it painful realizing that she wasn't really there—that she was a projection? But you found a way to break through, didn't you? Like a fallen angel, you separated from the universe of what you perceived to be tormentors. And forged your own of anguish and subjugation."

"No, Cosden!" he shouted. "I've created a world of order and purpose that evades your meaningless and aimless subsistence. I've moved through all of human history, injecting order where you created chaos. I've improved upon your work. And as I grow more powerful, I will outpower even you."

"When will that happen?" Cosden asked him.

"I think you and I both know that happens tonight. Not even the personifications that surround you can stop me."

Cosden looked to Hosuto and Kokoro and The Professor, all of whom remained silent. Then he turned his gaze back to The Dark Man.

"I've just realized the most vital piece of information to the puzzle that consumes you and me," Cosden said to him.

"What might that be?" he asked.

"I have realized that I am the creator, the begetter, the sustainer. That makes you the destroyer, John."

"Is that truly how you feel?" The Dark Man scoffed.

"It is."

"Then you are truly a fool, unworthy of the very universe you formed. You see, you've got it all wrong, Mister Ke. I'm not the destroyer. I am the maintainer. Make no mistake, I will dismantle. But I dismantle out of necessity. Only through destruction can reconstruction begin. That is where I enter the picture. I will further deconstruct all you have built and reconstruct in *my* image."

"You don't have the power to do that," Cosden said.

"But *you* do, don't you? The Absolute, The Supreme Mind, The Demiurge, The Sustainer. Oh great creator. Am I not worthy enough?"

"This is not about worth. It has never been about worth. It's about amity, altruism, harmony. Of which you have none. Nor do you have the power to defeat me in any capacity."

"Are you sure about that?" The Dark Man asked. And immediately rows and rows of faceless police officers appeared from nothingness and surrounded them and encircled them.

"How about now?" The Dark Man laughed. "Still sure?"

Cosden looked around at each of the tall, pale, faceless figures and remained calm. They were surrounded by hundreds, if not thousands.

"Are these all of you?" Cosden asked him.

"All of me? No. There's still quite a few more."

"I assume it will take all of you to defeat me," Cosden said smugly.

"If that's what it takes. You know, Cosden Ke, it's about time you learn just how infinitesimal you really are. Your Professor and pals have rushed to stroke your ego at every turn. So desperate for a messiah, they've never stopped to question if you're really who you say you are."

"But you know that I am exactly who I say I am. Or else a thousand of you would not be surrounding me right now, would you?"

"That's one way to look at it. Another way to see it is to understand that I'm a careful man who doesn't like to take chances. Not when the universe is at stake. I'm afraid it ends tonight, Mister Ke."

"You plan to kill me?"

"For now, I need you, Cosden. I need your physical embodiment. It's quite dreadful I'm afraid, but I'll need you catatonic—until I can figure out how to outrun this universe. When I can get to another universe that isn't controlled by the processor that is your mind, then I will eliminate you. In the meantime, I will enslave you—control you."

"You know I can't allow that," Cosden told him.

"Then destruction it is."

The countless Dark Men assumed a fighting stance as Hosuto pulled out his sword, Kokoro's hands lit with beams, and The Professor held up his fists.

"We're right beside you, Cosden," The Professor told him.

"For every honor of life," said Hosuto.

"Until the end," Kokoro agreed.

"I'll make you a deal," The Dark Man spoke again. "I'll allow them to live if you come with me, Mister Ke. If you give in, right away. You have a choice. You can neither continue to battle nor withdraw with anguish. But to give up and let go. Allow us to rule as we were meant to."

"No," Kokoro said. "Don't do it."

"We won't leave your side," said The Professor, his fists still raised.

"You heard them," Cosden said.

The Dark Man sighed. "Have it your way."

A thousand faceless figures swarmed them. They fought off the pale men left and right while long arms transformed into slashing blades. Cosden sent lightning bolts crashing through the stainless glass ceiling of the train station. The bolts electrocuted several of the figures in succession as they dropped to the ground.

The tide turned when the only figure with a face hurled a bright orb at Cosden. It hit him so hard that Cosden fell to the ground—pain, agony, possible defeat. Unable to move his back or legs, he watched as a faceless figure stabbed The Professor.

"NO!" Cosden yelled as The Professor fell to the ground. Cosden outstretched his arm to no effect. No telekinetic ability of any sort occurred. Then he watched as Hosuto fought off several of the faceless figures. But he too succumbed to their vast numbers. They slashed Hosuto's chest as he dropped dead. At last, Cosden watched as they overpowered Kokoro. She, too, was killed by the many Dark Men.

"No… No… No!" Cosden yelled over and over.

And then the figurehead hovered over him.

"You've lost, Mister Ke."

Cosden's eyes fluttered and finally he fell unconscious. He could feel his spirit leave the train station. The next thing he recalled, he woke up in darkness. Everything around him was pitch black—except a small glowing orb beneath his feet. Otherwise, he was floating in darkness.

He began to weep. He wasn't sure where he was. He only knew that he had lost to The Dark Men. And everyone he cared about had perished at their hands.

Wiping the redness of his eyes, Cosden watched a glowing figure draw near. Long beard, thin figure, brown robes—it was The Time Keeper.

"How are you, Cosden?"

"Time Keeper… Where am I? What is this?"

"It's the beginning of all there ever was in the universe. Here we are, at the very beginning."

"What has happened? What have I done?"

"You allowed your friends to die for you."

"I'm afraid you did, Cosden. I recall it quite vividly. The Dark Man asked you to turn give yourself up. You refused, you allowed Kokoro and The Professor and Hosuto die in your battle."

"That wasn't my intention."

"I'm sure it wasn't. But your body remains with them."

"Who?"

"The Dark Men. They possess your physical self and when you wake up, your spirit will be back in their possession as well."

"What do I do?" Cosden asked him.

"You tell me."

"I don't know. I can try to take out as many of them as I can when I wake up. When I'm back there."

"No use, I'm afraid."

"Why?" Cosden asked.

"Because the essence of your power arrived from knowledge. And who was the personification of knowledge?"

"The Professor," Cosden answered.

"That's correct. And without The Professor, your knowledge of power is no more. Your ability to move and bend and contort objects with your mind alone no longer lies with you. Such attempts will be rendered useless, I'm afraid. And that is precisely what The Dark Men desire."

"I can't stop them."

"At this point, I don't believe so."

"So I've lost?" Cosden asked.

"They will take you to a subterranean cavern. That is where they will all be present. There they will extract the rest of you—Okami, then me. They will kill us both. They will grow in number and engross the universe in darkness where you once brought light."

"No," Cosden demanded. "There must be something else I can do to stop them."

"Not with the choices you have made, I'm afraid. I'm sorry Cosden."

"No," Cosden refused to accept what The Time Keeper was telling him. "What if I can reverse the choices I've made?"

"Yes?" The Time Keeper said.

"Kokoro told me that choices are not static. I believe her."

"In believing in others, you can trust their light to lead your way. And trust is something The Dark Men will never have."

"I just have to reverse my choice," Cosden said. "But how?"

"Am I not The Time Keeper?"

"You can help me!" Cosden grew excited. "We can save them."

"We can," The Time Keeper smiled. "It is a forgone

conclusion that I simply needed you to arrive at."

"We can reverse time! I can save The Professor and Kokoro and Hosuto!"

"When you awaken," The Time Keeper told him, "they will withdraw the spirit of Okami from within you. Then they will come for me. I'll use every ounce of my strength to compel them. That is when you will use my dominion as your own in order to turn back time. From there, it will be up to you."

"But will they be expecting it?" Cosden asked.

"No," The Time Keeper answered. "As beings of order, they never expect a change in plan. Having killed your physical personifications, they already believe themselves to have won. They will take you underground."

"That is when we'll do it."

"You must be swift," The Time Keeper nodded to him. "The window to act will not be wide. If they kill me first, it cannot be done."

"I won't fail you. I won't fail any of you."

"Are you ready, Mister Ke?"

"As ready as I'll ever be."

"Then let our plan for salvation commence."

In a single flash of light, Cosden's spirit was thrust through space. He opened his eyes and the next thing he knew, he was being strapped to a standing steel gurney by several faceless figures. He fought against them but they overpowered him and forced his arms and legs into binding straps.

Cosden looked around the massive subterranean cavern. It was a vast enclosed space covered with faceless figures. There were thousands upon thousands of them, standing shoulder-to-shoulder. Then they split apart like the red sea as their speaker walked through the crowd and made his way to Cosden.

"Here we are, together again, Cosden," said The Dark

Man. "But not the way you expected, I'm sure."

"I'm going to get out of here. And I'll do to you what you won't do to me."

"Oh, I don't think so. Make no mistake, Cosden. I plan to kill you, but I'm going to take my time. I think I'll strip you of your memories. And what are memories but the very stuff that make us who we are? But before taking your memories, I think I'll start with your knowledge—The Professor's already gone. So insignificant, so pedantic. I'm happy I'll never have to hear his voice again."

"He'll be back, I promise."

"Why would you say such a thing? Do you have the power to resurrect? I don't think so. I think you're stalling, buying time. The Professor is gone for good and you and I both know it. I think you're afraid of facing reality. I think you're afraid of what I'm going to do."

"Where are we?" Cosden asked him.

"We're underneath the train station."

"Are all of you here?"

"Yes," The Dark Man answered. "Each and every one of me is here. No one wanted to miss this."

"So this is where you've always gathered? This is where you return. The spot where it happened."

"What?" The Dark Man asked with confusion.

"Where the bright light took your mother, John. Above us is the train station where it happened. And this is where you gather."

"Lies!" he yelled.

"If the story is a lie," Cosden said, "then why does it upset you so? You know what I think, I think it's all true, John."

"You're trying to get under my skin, Cosden."

"You think that I'm the light—the light that took your mother. It wasn't me, John. But I know that explaining this to you won't change your perception. Nothing can do that.

You are truly lost."

Cosden looked into The Dark Man's eyes and could see a hint of truth to what he was saying. He knew he was correct.

"Enough!" The Dark Man yelled. "I'm not sure what kind of pathetic tactic you're pulling but I will put up with no more of it. I'm going to destroy you, Cosden. Here and now."

"Then what I said earlier was true."

"Eh?"

"That I'm the sustainer and you are the destroyer."

The Dark Man held his hand out and forced it into Cosden's chest as if his hand were a hologram. The light emitted from Cosden's chest and from it The Dark Man withdrew the transparent spirit of Okami. Using only one hand, he held Okami into the air by the neck.

Then he snapped Okami's neck. The spirit faded and wilted away as thousands of Dark Men watched silently.

"One more down," The Dark Man said. "And I once liked that one. Before you got to him. One more to go."

The Dark Man's hand reached into Cosden and turned transparent once more. This time an even brighter light emitted from him. From the light, The Dark Man pulled his fist away and realized he was holding onto the neck of The Time Keeper.

"You're next," The Dark Man said to him.

The Time Keeper grabbed The Dark Man's hand and forced it from his neck. The other Dark Men began to run and scramble as The Time Keeper sent a cylindrical blast that knocked them all to their feet.

"Now Cosden!" The Time Keeper yelled. "Go now!"

Cosden closed his eyes and a whirlpool of light began to engulf him. He had formed a vertex that sped around him fast and faster until suddenly, he disappeared from the subterranean cavern. The next thing Cosden knew, he looked up and found himself standing in the train station. Right ahead of him was The Dark Man and behind him was Kokoro, The Professor, and Hosuto. They were all surrounded by hundreds of Dark Men.

Cosden had traveled an hour into the past and was now reliving the same moments.

"Then destruction it is," The Dark Man said to Cosden.

Just as it occurred the first time, the countless Dark Men presumed a fighting stance as Hosuto pulled out his sword, Kokoro's hands lit with beams, and The Professor held up his fists.

"We're right beside you, Cosden," The Professor told him.

"For every honor of life," said Hosuto.

"Until the end," Kokoro agreed.

"I'll make you a deal," The Dark Man spoke the same words as he did the first time Cosden experienced this moment. "I'll allow them to live if you come with me, Mister Ke. If you give in, right away. You have a choice. You can neither continue to battle nor withdraw with anguish. But to give up and let go. Allow us to rule as we were meant to."

"No," Kokoro said. "Don't do it."

"We won't leave your side," said The Professor, his fists still raised.

Cosden thought for a moment and refused to repeat the same answer. "Yes, you will," he told them.

"What?" Kokoro asked.

The Dark Man appeared puzzled.

"I don't want to lose each of you," Cosden said. "You don't understand it right now, but if you fight next to me, it will only be my fault. I can't allow it."

"With all due respect," said Hosuto, "we are not leaving."

"I'm afraid you are, Hosuto. Each of you."

Cosden turned around to face his friends. He extended a hand out and all three of them instantaneously dematerialized out of view.

"Very interesting, Mister Ke. Very noble—even for you," The Dark Man laughed. "Are you really just giving in? I proposed it but I was sure you would be too arrogant to agree."

"I guess I can surprise even you, John."

"No matter."

With all of his companions gone, Cosden was prepared with a new strategy. But before he could do anything else, The Dark Man sent a blast of light at him that knocked him to his feet. Just as he had the first time around, Cosden dropped to the floor and fell unconscious. He awoke without a single sense of how much time had elapsed. He was being strapped to the standing steel gurney. He was in the same massive subterranean cavern, surrounded by thousands of Dark Men as their personification made his way through the crowd.

"We're all here, Mister Ke. Each and every one of me," he said to Cosden as he faced him. "I just keep wondering. Why? Why? Why? *Why* would you dispose of your own companions? What are you without them after all?"

"I've sent them to a safe place. And once I'm free from here, I'll meet them again."

The Dark Man laughed. "You'll never be free from here and you'll never be free from me, Cosden. Not until death has taken you."

"I know you won't believe me, and perhaps that's why I'm telling you in the first place. But I've already experienced this. I know your every move. I know what you're thinking and I know how you feel. I know that we're under the same train station that your mother perished at. I know that you blame me for that. You think that it was I who took her from you. But you're wrong, John."

"You are truly insufferable, Cosden Ke."

"I know precisely what you're going to do next," Cosden said calmly. "What I have not experienced, however, is how this will end. I can only ascertain that your demise occurs tonight, and with it, the emergence of peace in this universe. Of that, I am certain."

"Enough!" The Dark Man yelled as he reached his hand back. But when he drove his arm toward Cosden, his fist stopped in mid-air. A luminous forcefield was surrounding Cosden and it prevented The Dark Man from touching him.

"What's this!?" The Dark Man said angrily.

The thousands of pale faceless figures that surrounded them assumed a position that indicated they were mounting an attack. But before they could act any further, a cylindrical wave reverberated from Cosden. The blast hit every figure in the room and knocked them over.

The figurehead of The Dark Men was bent over, coughing, and screaming from the agony of a deep penetrable ringing in his ears.

"What have you done!?" The Dark Man screamed.

Cosden looked at the straps that bound him to the gurney and they immediately released him. He calmly stepped down from the steel gurney as if all the time in the universe were at his disposal. Then, as the thousands of faceless Dark Men screamed from the dense ringing, Cosden formed a ball of light in his palm. The light contorted itself into a lustrous and radiant sphere. Cosden placed the sphere on the ground and rolled it over to the only other man in the room with a face.

"What is this!?! *No! No!*" The Dark Man screamed again.

Cosden lifted his head up and peered upward. The ground rumbled and shook. Then he rose into the air and shot through the top of the cavern. He shot up through floor of the train station and then through the stainless glass windows of the terminal's ceiling. Cosden was floating in the sky as he looked down below.

In the cavern, The Dark Man grabbed the glowing sphere and it emitted a nuclear blast that destroyed everything in sight. The entire subterranean cavern collapsed upon itself as fire blazed through the train station. And it too collapsed to the ground as heat waves and flames engulfed everything in sight.

Cosden continued to witness the catastrophic calamity while the sun re-entered the sky and brought day where there was darkness. He flew off as the fire rose with the sun's rays. Moving as fast as light through cold clouds, Cosden flew over several cities until he made it to a tall, seemingly limitless, forest. In the forest he descended from flight. There he was greeted by The Professor.

"I like what The Clinician has done to the forest," Cosden told him. Then he walked over to a small plant; it was the tree of life that Cosden planted after defeating Okami.

"She works wonders," The Professor smiled. "And she returned our estate back to pitch perfect condition. Who needed a fortress after all?"

"The tree of life here grows quite preciously, doesn't it?" Cosden asked. "I trust it with you and The Clinician far more than I trust it with even myself."

"That's rather flattering, Cosden. But in fear of turning a topic where it isn't headed…"

"Feel free," Cosden told him.

"Then I must ask, did you defeat him?" The Professor asked. "Are The Dark Men no more?"

"Yes and yes," Cosden answered.

"I can but say that news is most excellent and pleasing to the senses," The Professor smiled softly. "I am glad to hear it."

"Where are the others?" Cosden asked.

"Inside. We thought you'd succeed so we took the liberty

of preparing a small hurrah."

"I'm out defeating the forces of evil and you all are planning a party," Cosden laughed.

"Sounds about right," The Professor said. "I knew sooner or later you'd realize that the role of begetter and the absolute has its disadvantages."

"I'm not complaining," Cosden smiled.

"Not yet!" The Professor laughed. "Give it a bit more time."

"It's nice," Cosden said. "Peace is. Seeing it, hearing it, living it."

"Thank you for saving our lives, Cosden."

"You know what happened?"

"The Clinician filled us in. I suppose it why we knew we needn't worry."

"I was looking forward to telling that story myself," Cosden chuckled.

"Cosden?"

"Yes, Professor?"

"Have I ever explained to you the flame and the moth?"

"No, Professor. I don't believe you have."

"There are two distinct types in this world. First is the flame, the originator of light and warmth. Infinite is its attraction due to the necessity of its practicality. So powerful, in fact, is the flame that it is the only element capable of forging steel into any configuration known to man. So beautiful is the flame that only the most exquisite mincrals, known as opals, may borrow its namesake. And then there is the moth. You see, the moth is merely the creature most captivated by the flame."

Side by side they walked through the forest, with the knowledge that tomorrow would arrive with more harmony than yesterday.

Afterword

Several years ago, my brother proposed an idea to me. "What if I'm not real? What if nothing is real? How can you be sure that anything exists outside of your own mind? Maybe everything else is a projection. That's a real philosophy, y'know?" So powerful was this notion that it remained with me, even if I didn't fully believe it. But there it was, always niggling and philosophically gnawing at me. Then I read about this theory again and found a name for it—Solipsism—espoused by the great philosopher René Descartes and even mentioned briefly by Sigmund Freud himself (thus the opening quote of this book). This philosophy is also commonly referred to as "Brain-in-a-vat theory." It configures that "in the beginning" (my words) our brains lie in a jar and electrical impulses send signals to the mind that forge the illusion, perception, and projections that make up our reality. If that one line does not explain this theory, as it ought to, please google "Brain-in-a-vat," you'll be glad you did.

Over a year before beginning the manuscript, I came up with a funny idea. *Why not turn solipsism into a book?* I jotted down the mere idea in a notebook and assumed such an undertaking, with its philosophical and theoretical underpinning, would be too daunting. But a year later, I woke up one morning and realized that it had to be done. While my writing process is generally to plan in great detail, chapter-by-chapter, that was not done with this book. Perhaps because there are no chapters in this book! That was quite purposeful. I want this novel to be read and experienced in one fell swoop. No breaks, no stops, no distractions to put it down. I almost see this book as one long chapter. But it remains purposefully short in comparison to other 21st century novels, where 600-page tomes have become the norm. I did not want to do that with this story. I can already see it now. The meaningful and dense dialogue of this book will be considered by some to be too dense. So can you imagine 600 pages of this? Heads would explode. I prefer to exert the notion that 160 pages of my short novel, an exercise in esoterica, will be just as worthwhile as any longer manuscript. I have admittedly packed a great deal of material into this book. And I hope, dear reader, you will enjoy experiencing this book as I enjoyed writing it. Who knows? If sales are ripe, we may get to join Cosden and The Professor once more. I will simply leave you with the tagline that I conjured up for this story.

Solipsism cannot be explained. It can only be experienced.

I hope you enjoyed,
A.L. Patterson